Lone Star Blood

Another Volume of the Entertaining and Mostly If Not Always True
Adventures of Texas Ranger Jim Reade and his Blood-Brother
Delaware Scout Toby Shaw
in the Time of the Republic of Texas

A Diversion by

Celia Hayes

Watercress Press
San Antonio, 2023

A *Watercress Press* book
from Geron & Associates
www. watercresspress.com

ISBN-13: 978-0-9897823-9-5
ISBN-10: 0-98923-9-5
Cover design by Watercress Press

A Note, with Acknowledgments, and Dedication

This series is my own creative attempt to breathe new life into a narrative which started as a radio serial, morphed into a TV series and then into a movie which turned out to be ... not what had been hoped for, even with Johnny Depp camping it up. When the movie came up in an internet conversation with some fellow writers, I argued that perhaps the best way to relaunch the franchise would be to ditch the mask, the silver bullets, etc., then rack it back to the independent nation of Texas in the 1840s and make it more or less historically accurate, using all manner of real history, Texas folklore and legend. And so I did – and it was enormously good fun, as well as popular with fans of the Western genre – a genre which is not dead in the least, as much as the mainstream publishing industry would like to make it so. I should note that the short adventures in *Lone Star Sons, Lone Star Glory,* and *Lone Star Blood* do not follow a strict chronological time-line, but they all take place during the time that Texas was an independent republic, under the presidency of Sam Houston, Mirabeau Lamar, and Anson Jones

Finally, this book is dedicated to the memory of two gone before me: my father, Page Hayden, and my late business partner, Alice Geron of Watercress Press. I continue with fond memories of their affection and support.

Celia Hayes
March, 2023

Contents

1 — THE FIRST ADVENTURE: THE MATTER OF JEDIDIAH 1

2 — THE SECOND ADVENTURE: THE KING OF KIBERA 47

3 — THE THIRD ADVENTURE: THE HAUNTING OF BELL HOUSE 79

4 — THE FOURTH ADVENTURE: THE DEATH OF A DISAGREEABLE MAN 125

5 — THE FIFTH ADVENTURE: TWO HOUSES, ALIKE IN DIGNITY...............................153

NOTES — LONE STAR BLOOD..183

1 – The First Adventure: The Matter of Jedidiah

Wherein Jim and Toby are assigned to protect the heir to a prosperous house in East Texas – a very unusual heir!

"Well, Jim," said Captain Hays one summer evening, as they sat outside the front door of the small adobe house off of San Antonio's central plaza, enjoying the cooler temperatures which fell as soon as the sun was well-down and a light breeze stirred the air, which discouraged mosquitos. "I have a curious assignment for you and Mr. Shaw as the pair of my stiletto-men currently at liberty – and this one might even call upon your skills as a man of law."

"As long as it doesn't depend on my sharp-shooting ability," Jim Reade replied, and his commander laughed, wry laughter. "Where need we travel to on the occasion of this mission, and with what duty are we being charged?"

Across the plaza, the light from lanterns hung swaying in the trees above the tables where the chili-selling vendors hawked their wares. A thread of music from a trio playing guitar, fiddle and concertina, hung in the air like the smoke from the chili-vendor's cook fires. The old town of Bexar came alive after sundown, when the heat of the day abated.

"A plantation a little west of Richmond," Jack Hays leaned back in the leather and stave Mexican chair, and drew on his pipe, sending a small spiral of tobacco smoke upwards. "Pecan Grove; established in the earlies by one of Austin's first three hundred settlers. A Scot named Josiah Malcolm, emigrated in his youth from Perth, settled in the Carolinas and made a small fortune, then took up land in Austin's grant and made another. He died about five years ago, leaving the entire estate to his wife, Mrs. Ada Malcolm. General Sam always had a soft spot for Mrs. Malcolm, since they were neighbors for a time. The situation is now Mrs. Malcolm has died … and in the will, she willed everything, lock, stock, and barrel to a certain beneficiary. General Sam has asked me privately, if I could send someone to safeguard the life of that beneficiary."

"And there is someone contesting the will?" Jim Reade asked. "Were there no natural heirs to the property, who would inherit if there were no will?" This certainly sounded intriguing. He was aware, in a manner of speaking, of Pecan Grove Plantation, and of Ada Malcolm as a redoubtable woman of strong character.

Captain Jack Hays shook his head. "There was a son, but he was the supercargo on a China clipper lost at sea, as I understand, about eight years ago. Great tragedy, as all their hopes were invested in him. The person contesting the will and threatening the life of the beneficiary is a nephew, the son of Josiah Malcolm's younger brother. A feckless, useless sort of man. I've met him a couple of times. A gambler and unlucky at it, which you'd think would be an inducement to give up games of chance, but Hake Malcolm is even more stupid than he is unlucky. Always coming round to touch up his uncle for a loan. Old Malcolm used to indulge him for the sake of the family, but Mrs. Ada put a stop to it, as soon as she gained absolute control of the purse-strings and did Hake Malcolm resent that! Told everyone who would lend him their ears for five minutes, about what a miser she was, to flesh and blood..."

"Technically, she was not of his flesh and blood, but to her husband" Jim pointed out, and Jack agreed with a nod.

"Anyway, General Sam was fond of her, and he's never been accused of being ungallant to any woman, save perhaps his first wife. He's tied up with the Legislature in session for a few months, and he had a letter from the Malcolm family lawyer regarding the estate and the beneficiary."

"And he's worried about the Malcolm beneficiary?" Jim hinted, and Jack Hays nodded again.

"Well, he is the President, after all," Jack drew on his pipe. "The one who trusts us to deal with interesting and delicate matters. The beneficiary of a substantial estate being in danger from a resentful man who gives every indication of contesting the will, or even attacking the beneficiary with murderous intent is as delicate a matter as they come. There's just one thing..." Jack waited for Jim to rise to the bait. Jim didn't, at first. Jack was always holding back a key bit of information as a tease.

Finally, Jim said, "So, is there something we should know about this beneficiary which we are to protect, for the honor of General Sam and the nation of Texas?"

"Why, yes there is," Jack replied. "The beneficiary whose life may be in danger is a tame macaw named Jedidiah."

"You can't be serious," Jim exclaimed. "She left the entire estate to a bird!"

"Not just any bird," Jack knocked the spent tobacco out of his pipe and filled it again. "But a tame talking macaw. Magnificent bird, by the way. It was a present from her son, on his last visit before he was lost at sea. She and Josiah doted on the bird. They live sixty or seventy years, you know. And as far as I know, Jedidiah the Macaw hasn't named an heir."

"The management of Pecan Grove is in the hands ... er, the clawed feet of a macaw," Jim sighed. "I can hardly wait to see Mr. Shaw's face when I tell him about this assignment. Save that I believe he thinks most white people are a bit mad anyway."

"According to the Malcolm's lawyer," Jack replied, "Management of the household and estate itself is in the hands of an experienced and trusted man of business and the plantation overseer. Mrs. Malcolm left directions that all is to be managed as it was when she was alive. Jedidiah the Macaw lives a life of considerable comfort – luxury, even – just as he did when Mrs. Ada Malcolm was alive. Only now he is the titular owner of Pecan Grove."

* * *

Toby Shaw was, as Jim had expected, mildly amused at the scope of their new assignment, although Jim finally sighed, when they were some distance west of Richmond on the Brazos, riding along on the old Spanish high road between Bexar and the East.

"At least Jedidiah the Macaw hasn't been named to serve in the Legislature," he said, "As the mad Roman emperor Caligula named his horse as a senator."

"Indeed?" Toby's face bore an expression of incredulous scorn. "There is some deeper matter going on here, James. That a woman with charge over a property of such wealth as we speak would do such a curious thing. She was not notably deranged in her wits, was she?"

"Not that I had ever heard, and General Houston himself counted her as a worthy friend. The plantation of Pecan Grove is, by any account, a well-run and profitable enterprise. If Mrs. Malcolm was addled in her wits, she must have hidden it very well. Anyway, when we get to Richmond tomorrow, we are to meet first with the Malcolm lawyer, Mr. Patrick Chevallier, Esquire, who is supposed to brief us both regarding the strange situation. It is sincerely hoped," Jim added, "That Lawyer Chevallier will tell us more regarding the threat to the beneficiary of Mrs. Malcolm's will, and who may be held responsible for so serious a threat that General Houston was obliged through chivalry to be involved."

The two of them idled their way along at a leisurely pace on the morning they intended to arrive in Richmond; the fields and pastures were already green with burgeoning growth, the streams and branches flowing with clear water, and the spreading oak and cypress trees brilliant with their spring livery. A scattering of wildflowers brightened the verge of the road with dashes of pink primrose, bright yellow asters and blue and white buffalo clover. This was so very different from the arid landscape of the borderlands, of the western desert, even the well-watered lands around Bexar, watered by several spring-fed streams and the river which wound its way through Bexar, like a ribbon. But even Bexar was not as lushly green as rich as the lands in that part of Texas which had long been settled by ambitious Anglo settlers, looking for a new start and prosperity in grants to them made by the entrepreneur, Stephen Austin in the decade before rebellion and the war for independence scoured the land.

It all looked to Jim as if this part of Texas had recovered from wars' alarms with commendable speed. Richmond was among the most long-established surviving towns – civilized and laid out in the American fashion, a town of straight streets, a grid meeting at right angles, set about with plain houses and businesses constructed of sawn lumber, many with porches and verandahs set under overhanging roofs. Those of the better-off class were painted in pleasing colors and set about with colorful gardens and towering oak trees. All very pleasant and civilized; the businesses were clustered around Front Street, which ran all the way down to the Brazos River. Jim looked for the sign hung out advertising the legal services of Patrick Chevallier, Esq. & Associates. This proved to be hung from a double gallery in front of a substantial building which housed a general store and a popular modiste and dressmaker on the ground floor, with the legal services of Lawyer Chevallier on the second. Jim and Toby left their horses tied to a convenient railing and climbed the staircase to the second gallery. At a polite rap at the door, and receiving no answer, Jim tried the knob. The door opened, admitting the two of them to a pleasant large chamber, lined with a wealth of bookcases and several desks, interspersed with a scattering of comfortable chairs and lighted by tall windows on either side of the door.

Obviously, the practice of Chevallier & Associates was a profitable one. The occupant of the nearest desk looked up at the sound of the door opening – a youngish man, with a shrewd countenance and little remaining hair, which was of an indeterminate color and slicked back across his skull. This made him look as old as Jim's father, although perceiving the lively expression in his eyes and the relatively unwrinkled countenance, Jim estimated Patrick Chevallier's age to be approximately half a decade older than his own, of twenty and six.

"James Reade, Esquire," Jim said by way of introduction. "Sent by Captain Hays, in the matter of ..."

"Jedidiah, the heir to the Malcolm estate," Lawyer Chevallier sprang up from behind his desk and advanced through the room to shake Jim's proffered hand with every evidence of welcome. "Thank God you have come! It is a very ... umm ... delicate affair. So reassuring that President Houston has taken such an interest in it. The Malcolms were respectable pillars of our little community ... and such very nice people," Chevallier confessed, with a touch of mild sorrow. He spoke in cultivated accents, which reminded Jim of his mother, who was a Yankee from New England. "I considered them and all of their people as the dearest of friends as much as they were clients. The matter of Jedidiah being the heir to Pecan Grove was a stopgap; a means of sheltering the estate and all of their people against a most dire threat."

"Posed by a resentful party, indignant at being passed over in the will?" Jim suggested. "Yes, we were briefed, but only in a cursory way. This is my associate and companion, my blood-brother Mr. Tobias Shaw, of the Delaware people, whose' able service and fine qualities are treasured by Captain Hays, almost more than my own," Jim added firmly, noting the brief hesitation with which Lawyer Chevallier extended the hand to Toby upon being introduced. "We were told that you would provide more information regarding this most peculiar behest."

"Indeed," Patrick Chevallier shook Toby's hand and gestured to the nearest group of comfortable chairs. "Well, if you would take a pew, I will attempt to outline the basic case. It is, as you have no doubt deduced, a stratagem to shelter the estate for a necessary time from the machinations of Hake Malcolm, a dissolute and impecunious gambler, of no notable traits of character other than to drink immoderately and gamble upon anything and everything that takes his fleeting interest – the number of petticoats that a popular tart wears, the winner of the latest horse-race or dog-fight, or the exact time of arrival of a steamboat."

"Of that we knew already," Jim replied, as he and Toby and Lawyer Chevallier settled into a trio of comfortable chairs arranged before the largest window, which overlooked the street below, and beyond it, the line of trees which delineated the riverbank. "I presume that Hake Malcolm is deeply in debt to various creditors. This is the most usual fate of unlucky gamblers. The usual stratagem employed by such is to leave town in search of greener pastures and more innocent creditors."

"Alas that the younger Mr. Malcolm did not take to that method," Patrick Chevallier sighed. "It would have saved a great deal of trouble and grief for Mrs. Malcolm. In any case, having a wealthy uncle, who could be appealed to for loans of small sums when Hake Malcolm was most financially embarrassed ... was his misfortune when it came to forming his character. It made it easy for him to continue in a dissolute way of life. When the elder Malcolm passed from this mortal coil and left the estate to the entire control of Mrs. Ada, she was not inclined to be indulgent. Mrs. Ada was adamant in her refusal to give him any more money. I believe with all my heart that she hoped that the shock of being turned off to fend for himself would have brought about a reformation of his character."

"It did not?" Jim hinted, for Chevallier seemed sunk in melancholy reflection, to be started out of those thoughts with that simple question.

"No, alas – it had the most opposite effect. Hake Malcolm was vociferous in his resentment. So abusive and unchivalrous with the regard to his aunt by marriage that certain men of Richmond threatened to horsewhip him in the street, after hearing him voicing such abuse in public. Mrs. Malcolm was an ornament to our small society in Richmond, gentleman ... but some of his creditors have since made themselves into his allies, on the promise that he would make good on his debts to them, once he had control of Pecan Grove."

"And Mrs. Malcolm was distressed at that possibility?" Jim asked, and Chevallier nodded.

"Most especially, since it had been not just her family home and enterprise over the last two decades, but also the home of their servants and field hands. Indeed, Pecan Grove has been the only home that all but the very oldest of them have ever known. I shared her fear that upon inheriting as the sole living next of kin, that Hake Malcolm would promptly break up the property and sell off the servants. She could not abide that thought; that people who had served her family so loyally, and for whom she felt deep affection would be wrenched from their home, that families would be broken apart, willy-nilly, and all in order to pay the debts owed to a worthless scoundrel. Personally, I hold no briefs for the peculiar institution of slavery," Patrick Chevallier regarded them with honesty. "Yet, it exists – until divine providence sees to the abolition of the vile system. As such, it is a reality, and one with which a thinking man, and a man of law must deal."

"Did Mrs. Malcolm consider manumitting the Pecan Grove slaves, as a possible solution to the dilemma?" Jim asked. Indeed, this would have been his own advice, if asked to consult in a similar case.

"This was my first thought," Patrick Chevallier replied, earnestly. "Some of the house servants, and one or two of the skilled – Persephone the housekeeper, Jubal the butler, and Cyrus the coachman, to name three – are possessed of sufficient savings to purchase their own freedom, and skills to pursue gainful employment, should it come to it. But being free men and women of color would hardly secure any personal safety for them. It has not been unknown that such free persons might yet be kidnapped, taken far away by unscrupulous persons, and sold again into bondage. Such notoriously unscrupulous men are the friends and confidants of Hake Malcolm. A free man or woman of color would be perceived by them as a bag of gold, walking around on two legs and free for the taking," Chevallier added, with an uncharacteristically bitter tone of voice. "Ironic indeed – known to be a piece of highly valuable property belonging to a rich estate is better protection for a person of African race than all the laws of the land! What a kind of freedom! In any case, the colored folk of Pecan Grove assured us that they would, in a phrase, rather hang together in the guise of bondage, with their friends of long servitude and sheltering their children, than be hanged separately on the scaffold of the peculiar institution."

"It is a curious matter," Jim agreed, his tone neutral, as befitting one given to uphold the law, and given authority by the nation of Texas. He deeply sympathized with Chevallier's abolitionist opinions, and the quandary in which such sympathies had placed him. His own parents shared such and only hired free men and women of color at their house in Galveston. But a household of two or three hired servants was a different situation, compared to a working plantation with forty or fifty workers, workers with families and a sense of belonging to the only home which most had only ever known. "What danger does Hake Malcolm pose to the beneficiary of Mrs. Malcolm's will, Jedidiah the Macaw?"

"An extremely dangerous one," Patrick Chevallier replied, his mouth set in a grim line. "He has made no secret of his enmity toward the late Mrs. Malcolm, and likewise no secret of his intention to gain the estate for himself by any means necessary. I had to secrete the original of Mrs. Malcolm's will with a trusted friend in Galveston, as my own office here was ransacked several weeks ago, in the middle of the night. Even an attempt to burn this building was made, not a week ago. Fortunately, Mr. Dunstable, who keeps the general store downstairs lives with his family in quarters behind the store, and he and his wife were able to raise an alarm and quench the fire. I have also been threatened directly by Hake Malcolm, but as you can see, gentlemen, I am not averse to defending myself ..." and he nodded in the direction of the ornate coat rack by the door, so that Jim and his blood-brother could see the brace of Colt patent repeating pistols which hung from a stout leather belt looped around one of the pegs. "I am no milk-toast scribbler of dusty documents, Captain Reade: my clients and myself are defended, both in the court of law, and in blood in the streets, if such is required."

"I wonder, if such is your determination to protect your late client's estate, why President Houston found it necessary to request our assistance, in an official capacity," Jim sat back in that very comfortable chair and regarded the older lawyer with puzzlement well-mixed with speculation. "It would seem that you have the situation with your client's estate well in hand."

Chevallier was already shaking his head.

"I am only one man, Captain Reade – and I have my other clients' affairs to tend. At the end of the month, the District

Court will sit, and Hake Malcolm has brought a suit to be heard, demanding that Mrs. Malcolm's will be overthrown. Not that it has any chance of success," Lawyer Chevallier added, with a rather smug air. "But there is considerable danger that in advance of the District Court hearing his case, that Hake Malcolm and his collection of sordid allies will attempt to make the whole point moot by eliminating Jedidiah the Macaw in a direct attack on Pecan Grove. And there is one more element in this case, on which you both should be advised..."

And Patrick Chevallier's voice lowered, in a conspiratorial manner, as he enlightened Jim and Toby, on that last interesting detail with regard to the Malcolm will, and disposition of the estate of Pecan Grove. At the conclusion of that whispered confidence, Jim regarded Lawyer Chevallier with astonishment.

"You are certain of this? What this person has claimed? It would change everything."

"That is the trouble," Patrick Chevallier replied, in regretful tones. "I am not. Neither was Mrs. Malcolm before her sudden passing. It was only one possibility and one which seemed exceeding remote when the first communication arrived from half the world away. How could we be certain, indeed? It seemed best to use our original strategy and wait on developments, but then Mrs. Malcolm's health failed utterly. Now there remain only weeks to go, in allowing this to play out. Am I assured of your assistance in this matter, Captain Reade?"

"Depend on it," Jim replied, firmly. "Depend on it, indeed."

Patrick Chevallier nodded in approval. Rising from his chair, he took down his hat from the rack by the door. "Then, gentlemen, if you are willing to extend your journey a trifle longer, I will guide you to Pecan Grove and acquaint you with the folk there; the overseer and business manager, Mr. Morris Tapley, Jonas the foreman of the field workers, Jubal the butler and Persephone the housekeeper, who was the late Mrs. Malcolm's confidant and nurse in her last days on earth. I should inform you that those four have formed a kind of leadership committee among the Malcolm folk. Jubal and Persephone have worked in the household for decades and were trusted implicitly by Josiah and Ada Malcolm. Even more so than some blood kin that I have known," Patrick Chevallier added, cynically.

* * *

Chevallier had a saddle horse, around at the back of his place of business. While he went to fetch it, Jim and Toby awaited him by their mounts at the hitching post.

"Interesting, your law regarding property," Toby remarked. "Among my folk, the women are the keepers of property – all property, save perhaps a warrior's weapons and the blanket that he sleeps in. Which is only logical, as they hold it for their children."

"Your folk have a different way of looking at familial matters," Jim replied, barely noting the black-bearded and heavy-set character with the aspect of an angry bull who advanced down the plank sidewalk toward them.

"It has been proven, time and time again," Toby retorted with an air of sagacity, "That any woman knows with certainty of a child which she has birthed, and a child also knows their mother, connected as they are by the birth-chord until it is severed ... but how certain might a man be of the children he claims as his? Unless he has kept his woman locked in a cage for all of the time that they are together. I do not think that any sensible woman would consent to that treatment from a mere man."

"Trust it is," Jim replied, this was an old topic of discussion between them. "A question of trust, in the vows sworn before God, to be faithful in marriage, to admit none other to the marriage bed other than the man and woman sworn to those vows. It's the difference between your people and mine."

"True enough," Toby agreed with a smile. "But at least, my people do not admit the injustice which happens among your people, when a woman might lie about who fathered her child. Among our people, a woman has no reason of gain to lie. She has the property and her children. They are hers, and the duty of her brothers is to do their part..."

At that moment Patrick Chevallier came around the corner of the building, leading his horse by the reins – an elderly, but fine-looking bay, obediently clumping after him.

"Chevallier ... you ...!" the black-bearded man had reached them, and his fury was obvious.

Patrick Chevallier looked the man up and down, commendably imperturbable, which spoke highly of his nerve. "Mr. Malcolm, do you have an appointment?" He asked, in mild tones. "I fear that I have an urgent appointment at the moment, but I can pencil you into my diary for a consult at eleven, tomorrow morning."

The black-bearded man replied with a volley of profane insult, his face growing redder and reader, to which Patrick Chevallier yawned, deliberately and for insult, while Jim and Toby watched.

"Really, Malcolm, you demonstrate the paucity of your education, and the relative lack of breeding, in bandying such terms in public. It's a wonder you are received by any respectable family in Richmond. Now, if you would be so kind as to get out of my way..." Chevallier smiled, a humorless and sharklike smile, and a small derringer appeared by magic in his fist, aimed directly at Hake Malcolm's lamentably garish brocade waistcoat. "I shall see you tomorrow at eleven in my office. I bid you good day, sir!"

"I'll call you out!" Hake Malcolm snarled, "S' help me God, I will!"

"When your courage ... as well as your marksmanship is equal to the challenge, I shall be more than happy to oblige," Chevallier replied, not the least bit perturbed. "My office at eleven ... or at dawn with your second, at the riverbank near to the big sandbar. Your choice, of course."

To Jim's mild astonishment, Hake Malcolm's rage-reddened countenance turned slightly paler. He shouldered past Patrick Chevallier, and Jim without another word.

"It looks as if I have no appointments tomorrow," Chevallier remarked, coolly. "No matter, Mr. Reade. I have better things to do than bandy words or bullets with scum such as Hake Malcolm. Shall we be on our way, gentlemen?"

There was nothing more to say, until they were nearly out of town. Jim, who rode companionably elbow-to-elbow with Patrick Chevallier remarked, "You are a remarkably dangerous man, Chevallier. You were able to quell a violent man like Hake Malcolm with words and a two-shot derringer. I would like to know the story if you would favor me with your confidence."

"Ah," Patrick Chevallier grinned sideways at Jim. "You see ... my profession, as practiced – has brought me in the way of fighting a number of duels. Nearly a dozen at latest count; and I have won every one of them. My experience has been that once one has established a fearsome reputation, only a very few of the most incorrigible and recklessly stupid are willing to enter the affray. Strange it is, gentlemen. Strange it is, indeed."

"Well, at least it has run off Hake Malcolm," Jim observed, and Patrick Chevallier chuckled.

"For the moment, Mr. Reade. For the moment. He has much to gain, should he succeed in removing the one entity who stands in his path ... and he might yet receive a favorable hearing when the District Court meets in two weeks."

Pecan Grove was but a short ride out to the northwest of Richmond, following the gentle, marshy loop of the river, through more of that green and fertile countryside. Eventually, the rough and rutted wagon track approached a track branching off from it. There was nothing much to distinguish the entrance to Pecan Grove, and when Jim made mention of the relative modesty of it all, Patrick Chevallier replied,

"No, to make a very great do with an elaborate gate and drive was much against Mr. Malcolm's pure Scots soul and inclination. The main house itself is rather modest. Comfortable and modest. Mr. Malcolm believed that the land and wresting a living from it were all the riches that his family required. He had ... really, rather austere tastes," Chevallier mused, although he added hastily, "Mrs. Malcolm did impose on him the necessity of living in something rather more elaborate than a simple dog-trot cabin of two rooms and a breezeway between, so the house that she insisted be built when they had achieved a degree of success with planting cotton, indigo and rice is at least the equal of their nearest neighbors."

In relative silence, the three men rode past cultivated fields turned lushly green – corn and cotton and other crops, tended here and there by field workers with hoes, and bent attentively to their work. Jim did note that many of them did straighten from their labors and wave toward the three horsemen.

"You are a welcome visitor, I take it," he suggested to Patrick Chevallier, who nodded in reply.

"Indeed. I see the folk of the Malcolm plantation as able and sturdy allies, against the machinations of a despicable rogue as Hoke Malcolm." Patrick Chevallier looked very earnestly at Jim. "Quite unprofessional to admit to such personal feelings; but I respected Mr. Malcolm as a man of his word, and the late Mrs. Malcolm was almost as a mother to me. The folk of the plantation which they cherished are as dear to me as kin. I would not see their trust betrayed, not while I have breath in this body."

"And those are persons of whom President Houston has taken an interest, however slight," Jim replied. "So, this matter is of importance to the nation. Honorable, hardworking, and loyal folk – no matter what condition, free or not, of whatever race – freedom and justice is due to them."

"It is good to hear you say so, Captain Reade," Patrick Chevallier answered, with a look of profound relief. "I had long feared that we had no allies, in an official capacity, in the effort to keep Pecan Grove in that condition in which Mr. and Mrs. Malcolm wished so profoundly for it to continue."

At the last bend in the well-beaten track between the fields, the three of them approached the main house – not a grand mansion in itself, but a generously apportioned house of two stories with a veranda and covered galleries all the way around, painted white with sage-green shutters. Tall windows stood open on both floors to admit the ever welcome and wandering cool breeze. A pair of large mastiff dogs with heavy collars around their necks lounged in a sunny patch of lawn, barely raising their heads to blink solemnly at the three travelers. Upon apparently recognizing Lawyer Chevallier as a friend, both dogs returned to sleep. A garden of colorful flowers and lush green foliage framed the house, tended by a couple of small boys with watering cans, who upon recognizing Lawyer Chevallier immediately dropped their watering cans. The taller of the two came running to meet the three travelers.

"Howdy, Mister Chevalier!" the boy beamed welcome all over his face, "We ain't seen you in weeks! We were thinking you were poorly in health!"

"Fit as a fiddle, Ulysses," Patrick Chevallier replied, as he swung down from his saddle and gave the reins to the boy. "Never you fear. I've brought these two gentlemen to meet with Mr. Tapley, and your ma and pa, and Jonas. They've been sent by President Houston, to see that Jeramiah is kept safe!"

"Oh, my!" the larger boys' eyes widened. "'Zat the truth! Say, I'll take the gentlemums' horses 'round to the stable. Hector – you run tell Ma an' Master Tapley that you are here."

"Tell your ma that we'll go to the office, after I have introduced Captain Reade and Mr. Shaw to Jedidiah, since his safety is the reason for this visit," Patrick Chevallier instructed Ulysses, who beamed a smile and obeyed, leading the horses away with confident authority, although the child barely came up to the nose of the smallest of their mounts. The smaller child, Hector, had already scampered, abandoning the watering cans. Meanwhile, Patrick Chevallier led Jim and Toby into the house by the front door, where they were met, by a tall Negro man of some years, clad in impeccable livery, who opened the door just as Patrick Chevallier put his hand to the brightly polished brass doorknob.

"Jubal!" Chevallier exclaimed. "These gentlemen are sent by General Houston to secure the rights and safety of Jedidiah

– so I wished that they be introduced to the object of their care and concern. They are ...” Patrick Chevallier added with a significant glance toward Jubal, “Sympathetic to our cause, and worthy of every courtesy which this household may extend toward them. Captain James Reade, Esquire, and his assistant, Mr. Tobias Shaw, representing the noble Delaware tribe. This is Jubal, who commands the household, as he did when Mr. and Mrs. Malcolm were alive.”

“Seh...” Jubal inclined his head with imperishable dignity toward Chevallier and his companions. “You are welcome to this house, our roof and our salt, such as it might be.”

“I am pleased to be of service,” Jim said firmly, and extended his hand to Jubal, who after a momentary hesitation, took and shook it firmly. “Mr. Chevallier has told me of how deeply Mr. and Mrs. Malcolm trusted their people. To do what I can to secure their lives and yours – I am honored to serve.”

“Thank you, seh,” Jubal replied. “And now – if you please, I will introduce to you to Jedidiah ... our master,” he added with a wry and half-concealed grin. “In a manner o’ speaking, that is.”

“In a manner of speaking, of course,” Jim acknowledged the humor, and the agreeably cynical glint in Jubal’s dark eyes. “A thin pretense, of course – but as it stands in law, it may serve well. Especially if it can be maintained, through every artifice at my command.”

“Certainly, seh,” Jubal now smiled, as if sharing a pleasant jest with a co-conspirator. “Now, let me conduct you to Jedidiah. He has a pleasant room, set with greenery, and wide windows."

"I'll be in Mr. Tapley's office," Patrick Chevallier murmured. "Morris Tapley ... he was a school friend of the younger Mr. Malcolm, who recommended him to his parents. He is also very attached to Pecan Grove. I consider him to be a most loyal ally." He walked briskly ahead of them, through a pleasant hallway, which seemed to lead from the front to the back of the house, past a generous curving stairway, with several doors on either side. James glanced into the first as they passed, for a brief glimpse of an airy dining room, with green brocade-hung walls matching the upholstered seats of a range of chairs set around a long table, gleaming with polish industriously applied. Jubal led them to the door opposite. This proved to be a parlor, another room arrayed with comfortable chairs, and a marble-topped table. There was no fire in the grate, but a painted screen of brilliantly colored flowers and peacock plumes. A fine oil portrait in a splendid gilt frame hung over the fireplace mantel; a young man in a jaunty nautical seaman's jacket, painted against a vista of ocean waves and louring gray clouds. He was not a particularly handsome young man, with a lock of auburn hair falling over his forehead and a lantern-square jaw, but the painter had caught something of an engaging and perhaps reckless character in his aspect.

Jubal noted Jim's momentary interest.

"That, seh, is Young Master Jedidiah Malcolm. Miz Malcolm had it painted after his return from the first voyage to China. After Old Master passed, and Young Master was lost at sea, she would talk to this-here painting every morning, as iffen he was still alive and would come back to Pecan Grove." Jubal shook his head, pityingly. "Miz Malcolm, she was certain-sure that Young Jedidiah was alive ... just wandering in his wits, mayhap. Somewhere in those heathen places in the Far East."

"A sad ending," Jim remarked. "And yet – there is something to be said for hope that does not die."

"It surely would have been better iff'n Young Jedidiah had come back," Jubal shook his head, sadly. "But he nebber has, in all these years. Miz Malcolm an' Old Master, they thought the world of him, so did allus folk here."

"Mrs. Malcolm did the best that she could, to shelter Pecan Grove," Jim replied. "And she never gave up hope ... hope that might soon be rewarded." He did not dare say anything more, for fear of raising false hopes.

It would all be resolved, one way or another in a week or two if what Patrick Chevallier had told him was true.

"Jedidiah lives in the Garden Room," Jubal led them toward another double door on the other side of the parlor, doors which he flung open, and stepped back a little way. "Through this way, gennelmen."

Jim was a little lost for words at first, upon stepping into the Garden Room; at his heels, Toby was also silent. The room beyond was filled with leafy plants in urns and pots, not a few of them being small trees and shrubs, taller than a man, lush, green, and tropical, some adorned with flowers. The floor was paved in smooth slate stones, and the far wall, facing the south was filled with many panes of window glass, the expense of which attested to the wealth of Pecan Grove Plantation. Late morning sunshine poured into the Garden Room. It was warm and humid in the Garden room; small puddles of moisture gave evidence that the plants were kept well-watered. An ornate brass stand, which held up a trio of three plates, topped with a vertical metal hoop the size of a barrel hoop sat in the middle of the room. Atop that hoop sat a brilliantly colored macaw, one claw clamped around the hoop while the other conveyed a slice of apple to its curved beak.

"Jedidiah," Jim brought himself to speak, acknowledging their avian host, and somewhat aware of the ridiculousness of this mission and encounter. "So very pleased to meet you, at last. Don't let me interrupt your repast, but my colleague and I are here at the request of the nation of Texas to secure your inheritance and your safety."

"Awwwk!" replied Jedidiah, agreeably and ate a bit of apple. Then he flapped away to another perch, half-hidden in the greenery by the window.

Jim very deliberately did not catch Toby's eye. The danger of them both bursting out in laughter at the incongruity of this exchange was too close. Instead, he said, "Then show us to Mr. Tapley's office, Jubal, since we have made our courtesy visit to the beneficiary of Mrs. Malcolm's will."

"Indeed, seh," Jubal at least maintained an imperishable dignity of expression. Jim endeavored to match it, as he followed the butler back through the Garden Room, the main parlor, and the hall, out to the separate cluster of tidy small buildings at the back of the main house. The one to which they were conducted was a two-pen cabin in the Texas fashion, neatly white-washed and with green shutters covering the tall windows in each portion. Jubal tapped politely on the nearest door, which stood half-open. A male voice from within bid them welcome, and the three men entered to find the tiny office already quite crowded: a very young and thin white man sitting at a secretary desk against the wall, Patrick Chevallier, a sturdy Negro man of middle age in working clothes and a woman with a fairer complexion yet still of African blood in the genteel dress and apron of a housekeeper, seated around a small table in the center of the room, with three more empty chairs arrayed close by.

"This is Mr. Morris Tapley, who keeps the books and oversees the general run of the plantation," Chevallier performed the introductions. "Jonas, the head of the field crew, and Persephone, who manages the household, with Jubal. I have taken the liberty of sending for refreshments."

"Purlie is bringing them directly," Persephone murmured. She shared a bench with Jubal, and Jim noticed that their hands sought each other.

Chevallier continued. "This is James Reade and Toby Shaw of the Texas Rangers – they are trusted agents of the State, sent personally by Captain Hays to secure the safety of Jedidiah, against the threat posed by Hake Malcolm and his threatened law action. Mr. Reade is not only a Ranger but qualified in law – so these gentlemen are uniquely well-suited to defending the security of Pecan Grove."

"Hake Malcolm has already directly threatened Pecan Grove," Jim said, and noted that Mr. Tapley, Jonas, Jubal, and Persephone exchanged significant glances. Good – they already knew of the threat of violence. "This very day. And he even did so, in my presence. But I promise that we will do everything in our power to maintain Pecan Grove in the state which Mrs. Malcolm wished it."

"I have seen that guest rooms are prepared for you," Persephone murmured, "On Mister Chevallier's assurance that you will be staying here until the matter is resolved."

"Our thanks for the hospitality," Jim replied, heartened by this gesture of support. Although he was certain that Toby would take his blankets and go to sleep in some sheltered nook amongst the trees. "I must ask – should violence be threatened by Hake Malcolm and his allies – what have we on hand to defend Pecan Grove?"

"It's a chancy thing, folks of color turning weapons on white folks," Jubal commented, and Jonas the field boss nodded in agreement.

"I have a pair of patent Colts and an old Brown Bess," Morris Tapley confessed, and was taken by a racking cough. Jim sighed; Tapley looked as frail as a consumptive. No, he would not be a sturdy support in the case of violence launched at Pecan Grove. It would all be up to himself, Toby and perhaps Patrick Chevallier.

"We have our field tools," Jonas rumbled. "A mort o' damage can be done with scythes an' machetes. An' colored folk know real well how to use 'dem."

There was a mild chuckle among all the folk gathered in Mr. Tapley's office. Jubal cleared his throat and added a comment.

"We have dose dogs. Hera an' Zeus. Yeah, they laze 'round like they ain't got no interest; dey like mos' people. But dey hate Hake Malcolm for sure. He came to visit one day, when dey were just puppies, an' he hit Hera ... an' Zeus jus' went fo' him, all teeth."

"We'll take our allies where we find them," Jim replied. "So – myself, Patrick Chevallier, Mr. Shaw, to back up the Pecan Grove folk. I think we need to work out a system of pickets and runners day and night – especially at night – to alert us all if anyone approaches with hostile intent."

"The boys, I think," Morris Tapley nodded to Jonas. "In pairs, an older with a younger to be a messenger and to spell each other."

"Since you know the grounds well, Jonas – you set them out as you see best, in places where they might watch from concealment the main road, or any of the tracks through the woods."

At that moment, a servant girl – a pretty girl with slightly paler complexion than the other servants came through the door to the office, bearing a tray with tea things, plenty of cups and saucers, and plates of shortbreads and small pastries.

"Thank you, Purlie," Mr. Tapley nodded toward the girl, as she set the tray on the table. At a nod from Persephone, Purlie poured tea into each cup, and distributed them to each. She murmured to Mr. Tapley as she handed his teacup to him, and something in their soft exchange hinted at a special

27

fondness between the two. *Ah*, thought Jim – *that would explain something of Morris Tapley's loyalty to Pecan Grove; loyalty to the place and affection for Purlie*. He hoped that circumstances would not judge and treat them ill for their sincere feelings toward one another. Now Jim said,

"Mr. Shaw and I will review and work with any plan for trouble from Hake Malcolm and his allies. Which, since legal means have failed for him, may take the form of an open attack. Do you have any such plan for defense in existence?"

"Only to sound the alarm bell, and call for aid from our people, and all neighbors who can hear it," Mr. Tapley replied, and coughed again.

Jubal looked around at all at the table, with an air of magisterial authority. "We have seen off Hake Malcolm, when he came hisself, twice ..."

"Three times," Persephone murmured, and Jubal glanced at her in surprise.

"You nebber told me this, 'Sephony."

"No need," Persephone lifted her chin. "I saw him off by my lone self. I tol' him that he had no rights at Pecan Grove, an' he went, like the cur that he is. Purlie an' I were mopping the hallway. I threw a bucket of hot soapy water on him," She added by way of explanation.

"He might not go so readily, next time," Patrick Chevallier warned her. "This is why we must make plans to defend Pecan Grove – and the security of Jedidiah. Because, next time, he will come with allies. Armed allies with an inclination toward violence, determined to collect what is due to them, if Hake Malcolm gains control of Pecan Grove."

"So, in addition to putting sentries at some distance with messengers to bring warning, we must also contrive a place of safety for Jedidiah. I take it that everyone – and that would include Hake Malcolm knows that Jedidiah lives in the Garden Room?"

"A room with many glass windows and not easily defended, Brother," Toby pointed out.

"Exactly," Jim agreed. "Now ... where do you suggest that we take Jedidiah to hide him, in case of a direct attack on the main house."

"Our cabin," Persephone replied, without hesitation. "He knows Jube and me, real well – and he likes the boys, too. I don't think the high an' mighty Mr. Hake Malcolm will think to look for Jedidiah in the slave quarters."

"So we all hope," Patrick Chevallier commented. Meanwhile, Jonas cleared his throat.

"An' how long must we carry on like 'dis – keeping guard and ready? We have work to do in the fields, Mister Chevallier."

"I estimate two weeks, until the District Court meets, and Hake Malcolm's legal petition will be heard," Chevallier answered firmly, although from what he had privately told Jim and Toby at his office, the other man of law was being sparing with the absolute truth about the deadline. "Heard and rejected with the contempt that his suit merits."

"Two weeks," Jim mused, thoughtfully, and exchanged a glance with his blood-brother. "Two weeks. I believe that we can hold out for that long. Now ... this is what we will do." He added, and all heads at the table bent toward him attentively.

29

In the end, it was a whole ten days before Hake Malcolm and his allies made a move to threaten Pecan Grove. In that period, Jim and Toby began to feel somewhat at home there. As Jim expected, Toby made it his habit to sleep out of doors after dark fell, so that Jim could take the first watch as guardian, until the midnight hour, when Jim could cast himself – still fully-clothed save for his boots – on the bed in the small bedroom on the second floor, the one immediately over the Garden Room where Jedidiah lived in utter avian contentment, crunching his way through apples and corn and other food offerings. Patrick Chevallier spent his days in Richmond, and nightly returned to Pecan Grove in time to share a light supper, expertly prepared by Hebe, the cook, who turned out to be the full sister of Persephone and wed as the custom in the slave quarters was, by jumping over the broomstick with Jonas, the field worker's foreman. Patrick Chevallier brought with him the local newspaper and whatever interesting gossip came his way. Jim spent his own days and the first night watch walking the plantation boundaries and sorting out where any ambuscade of the property was likely to be launched.

Toby spent many of his waking hours with the Pecan Grove slaves. Being an Indian and a free man, but not quite considered as a white man, he had that entrée into their society denied to Jim and Chevallier, as fond and as respectful as the Pecan Grove folk seemed to be to them. He returned to the upper-story room given to Jim at one or two in the morning, so they might exchange the intelligence gained during their separate tours of vigilance and gossip-gathering, before Jim snatched a few hours of restless sleep while Toby patrolled the grounds.

"There is notice in the latest newspaper of an English ship now docked in Galveston," Jim reported. "A ship with a cargo of fine Chinese porcelain, and passengers. There was no word if said passengers were the ones which Patrick Chevallier was hoping for."

"We can hope, my brother," Toby replied. "Ah ... Hebe sent up fresh coffee for you. A white man's vice and habit, but I confess to being grateful for it."

"Supposedly, coffee was discovered by Arab herders, standing guard over their flocks in the wee hours ... and discovering that if they chewed the dried fruit and kernels of a particular plant, they might stay awake and alert." Jim felt obliged to dispense this bit of historical wisdom.

Toby laughed and added sugar to his own cup of aromatic dark brew. "Or to keep them awake and alert, while they plotted a raid on their neighboring rival's herd."

"I have no notion," Jim replied. "Only – I do believe that our nation runs on a plentiful supply of coffee, especially those who guard and guide. What bits of tasty gossip do you bring from the slave quarters?"

"That Purlie the serving maid is in love with Tapley the overseer and he with her. The elder servants are of a mixed opinion," Toby added sagely. "Some think she could better herself by passing for white and free, and going with him to some place where neither of them are known and marrying there ... but others believe that she is a fool, and he is taking advantage of her."

"He seems like an honorable man," Jim observed, and his blood-brother shrugged.

"If he is, or is not, it is nothing to do with our mission, James. In any case, he is not in good health."

"If Hake Malcolm and his friends are going to attack Jedidiah," Jim yawned widely as he pulled off his boots and carefully placed them where he might find them readily in the dark, "I really wish they would go and do it and get it over with."

Toby snorted. "Be careful what you wish for, James – for you might get your wish."

"Sooner rather than later," Jim moistened his fingers and pinched out the light of the single candle in the room. Toby chuckled and padded silently from the room. The door closed with a snicking sound behind him. Jim fell asleep almost before it did.

* * *

It hardly seemed a minute later that his blood-brother gently shook him awake. "You have your wish now, James. They're here."

Jim shot fully awake in a second. "Where? Are you certain?"

"Yes – young Ulysses and his brother Hector were watching the track which leads from the river. A band of men, twelve or fifteen with long rifles, their horses shod with rags, hoping to make a quiet advance from an unexpected direction."

"Is Chevallier awake?" Jim hastily pulled on his boots and buckled the belt with the holsters for his pair of Colt patent revolvers around his waist. "And the rest of the men?"

"All is as we had planned," Toby replied. "Mr. Tapley is directing the workers, as best he can, in the actions that we have suggested. Ulysses took Jedidiah to his parent's cabin for safety. Jubal says he will come up and load for us."

"Good," Jim approved. Patrick Chevallier and Jubal soon joined them on the gallery above the Garden Room, darker shadows than the dark of the gallery on a relatively moonless night. They waited, silently crouching, or kneeling on the gallery floor behind a row of urns and half-barrels full of plants and small shrubs.

There was a disruption to the normal tenor of night sounds – of crickets and other night-flying insects, and the distant peeping of frogs in the boggy places down by the river. The noise made along the track through the woods by a dozen horses and the men riding them could not be utterly silenced. Likewise, there were sounds within the house, of men and women trying to keep quiet, as they barred doors and windows against intruders; but still, floors creaked, and footsteps shuffled. Below Jim, Toby, and Patrick Chevallier, the hinges of a shutter screeched, as someone within drew it closed, the bolt shooting home, while a woman whispering urgently. The sounds of sibilant whispers carried in the nighttime silence. In the parlor on the ground floor, the tall clock chimed the half-hour. The house was alive – not deep in slumber, as the men approaching on horseback would have confidently expected at half-past four in the morning.

"They expected to strike just before dawn, in the manner of the Comanche, thinking that none here at Pecan Grove would be expecting an attack," Jim whispered, and bis blood-brother snorted in derision.

"There are men, my brother – who can be told a true thing and learn, and others who may read of a true thing and learn likewise. Then there are those men who must learn the true thing by bitter experience and much pain. Hake Malcolm must be one of that sort."

Jim repressed a chuckle, and so did Patrick Chevallier. Toby continued, in a perfectly serious voice. "Brother, we ought to attack the ambushers before they can do any harm. That would be the way of my people and prevent any harm to Pecan Grove and the people."

Both Jim and Patrick Chevallier shook their heads. "Legally, that would be indefensible," Jim explained. "They might claim that they were just casually riding past Pecan Grove, and we attacked them for no reason at all. We must wait until they make a move which can be read as violent intent."

"At just before dawn?" Toby whispered. "There is no good thing which happens at this hour, brother. Sometimes the customs of your law are puzzling."

"I know," Jim replied, glumly. "Ready, gentlemen – they're at the edge of the trees, now..."

Jim and Patrick Chevallier rested their sidearms on the edge of the sheltering plant urns, and Toby leveled the barrel of his own Baker rifle on the lowest urn; he lay flat on the gallery floor, making hardly any noise at all – as silent as a deadly catamount, waiting in ambush. The noise of men and horses, stumbling with many muffled profanities through the dark woods, in the faint light of a fading moon could not be hidden. If they had truly meant to attack a sleeping household, they might have gotten away with it, but at the moment when shadowy figures of men and horses emerged from the trees, Toby whistled loudly; a signal meant to sound like a night bird.

Among the mounted men, a torch flared into life, illuminating the trees, and sending the shadows dancing. Then another torch, and yet another, as the men in the trees spurred their horses out onto the lawn around Pecan Grove, shouting and whooping as they came.

"Now!" shouted Jim, and below in the house, a door opened, allowing the dogs to run out, snarling and baying as if they were the hounds of hell. Behind the house, the bell which rang for dire emergencies, such as fire or an Indian raid began to clang. A horse whinnied in terror, rearing as one of the canine shadows leaped at its rider, and the horseback raiders shouted in angry frustration. A fusillade of bullets shredded tree leaves and pattered like a deadly kind of hail against the house walls. Jim thanked their good fortune for the sturdy bulwark of plant tubs which they sheltered behind, and the imperturbable solidity of Jubal between himself and Patrick Chevallier. Also for Chevallier's proven and expert marksmanship.

The torch-bearing horsemen charged toward the house. Before Jim could get off a shot, the first horseman was below, having leaped onto the veranda below in one mighty effort from his mount and cast the flaming torch against the wall of the house.

"Open fire!" Jim whispered in a voice which barely carried to the defenders of Pecan Grove, and a wave of return shot sang out over the once-pleasant gardens and galleries. Jim emptied his first Colt revolver into the churning mass of riders and the horses which carried them and passed it to Jubal, wondering if his bullets had struck any target of consequence at all. He and Toby had briefed Jubal, had him practice reloading the finicky and fragile patent revolvers. This situation was different; stressful and under return fire, but Jubal carried on, precise and as careful as if he were going out a task in the management of the household which he ruled; counting and polishing the silverware or inventorying the contents of the wine cellar or china cabinet.

Below, in the once-pastoral and peaceful garden of Pecan Grove, their fire took deadly effect. There was a horse down, screaming in an unsettling and human-sounding voice, and at least two man-shaped figures, sprawled in an ungainly fashion on the mown lawn. Jim felt a pang of regret at this; killing another man, or having a part in killing, was not something which came readily to him. He could comfort himself, in the long hours and days afterwards, with the reminder that such a killing had been done in defense of the otherwise defenseless, and in the cause of justice – much that he would have wished that matters could have been settled otherwise. Hake Malcolm and his friends had chosen the path of violence and murder, rather than the path of peace and justice. He took his reloaded Colt from Jubal, assured that

Jubal had loaded it correctly with a brief glance, and sent off another fusillade into the seething mass of horses and men attacking Pecan Grove.

A single fallen torch burned sullenly on the dew-dampened grass. Jim was deafened by the sound of gunfire, especially by the blast of Toby's ancient Baker rifle, a weapon which Toby methodically fired and reloaded in a manner which would have given credit to a British auxiliary. Suddenly it was all over and done. Jim thought that three or four of the attackers had prudently withdrawn – with luck all the way to Richmond or beyond. There was one horse dead on the lawn, another thrashing feebly. The dark figure of a man sprawled next to the dying horse, clutching his leg and moaning curses to the unfeeling world. The sudden silence was as deafening as the storm of battle had been.

"We drove 'em off, for sure," Jubal grinned mirthlessly, his teeth a white slash across his face, blackened doubly by powder smoke. Even as he spoke, three women dashed out from the house with buckets of water, which they emptied over the dispirited flames licking at the veranda below, and on the discarded torches burning on the clipped lawn.

"Yes, this first time," Jim replied, as his mind ran ahead. "What if they come again and with determination, as the Mex army did against the Alamo fortress. Can Pecan Grove hold out for fourteen days?"

"We may have some relief before long," Patrick Chevallier replied, as he studiously reloaded his own armaments. "Trust me, Jubal – the law of this place will come to our aid."

"In the meantime, we must look to ourselves," Jim replied, wary and still slightly deafened from the volleys of gunfire. "Until we are certain that Hake Malcolm's friends will not return."

Toby lifted his head and sniffed the air. "I think not, Brother. It is nearly dawn. I do not think they will return."

"We did settle the hash of certain of them, didn't we?" Chevallier stood up and dusted the knees of his trousers.

"That we did," Jim answered, for in the east the sky was paling – the last of stars shining brightly before they were dimmed by the rising sun. "And now we have to sort out the butcher bill for it all."

He didn't relish the thought of having to dispatch the dying horse, even less than dealing with the wounded man. Given his own druthers, he would have preferred rendering medical aid to the horse and dispatching the man. Pecan Grove's alarm bell finally ceased ringing. With the rising of the sun, such danger as was posed by Hake Malcolm and his friends had been defeated for the moment.

Carefully holstering his loaded Colts, Jim ventured into the house and down the stairs into the main hall; which place was almost as dark as a Stygian tomb, with all the heavy shutters battened as firmly closed as if Pecan Grove was expecting one of those violent, windy fall storms – storms which swept in from the Gulf, bringing chaos, high water and toppled trees and structures in their wake. He fumbled his way through the spacious center hallway, and out the front door, where the light of a rising sun almost struck like a blow which blinded him temporarily.

When he recovered his vision, he looked out upon the gardens and lawn of Pecan Grove with wary satisfaction. The establishment had survived a direct and lawless attack. Jedidiah the Macaw was safely sheltered in Persephone and Jubal's cabin. Toby had gone to verify that. The house had been secured; none of the torches flung by the marauders had gained any purchase. The wagons rattling up the road must be those of the nearest neighbors and households, responding to the emergency. Jim walked over to the moaning man on the lawn, the one clutching his arm. It was Hake Malcolm, and the very picture of misery and defeat.

"You would have been better off accepting Chevallier's challenge," Jim remarked. "Pistols for two, breakfast for one. Ah, well, Mr. Malcolm – this is what comes from trying to take the law into your own hands. I would suggest that thereafter, you strictly confine your suits to the courtroom ... and refrain from taking matters into your own hands."

"You ...!" Hake Malcolm snarled, and Jim sighed, patiently.

"Do be polite, Mr. Malcolm, or we will just let you lie here and suffer unto death. Do you really, really want to take possession of a place where most all the folk will likely poison your food before you can sell it and them? Alas, I am a Christian, and we will take you up and bind your wounds, since all of your allies appear to have fled."

Jim gestured, resignedly, toward Jubal and Jonas, who fetched a shutter from the nearest side of the house and loaded Hake Malcolm onto it – not with any pretense of gentleness, and the man groaned again. There was no blood on his person, but his clothing was disarrayed and smeared with mud and grass-stains from the fall. Jim presumed that he had broken or sprained something when his horse went down. They carried him to the porch, just as a wagon came around the bend in the road, a wagon pulled by horses hastily harnessed and driven at a good clip. Jim didn't recognize the man at the reins, or the younger man who sprang from the seat beside him, but from the way that Morris Tapley and the Pecan Grove folk made them welcome, they were obviously not allied with Hake Malcolm.

"We came as soon as we heard the alarm!" gasped the young man. "Brought every bucket we had on the place, but it looks like it's all in hand! What happened?"

"Hake Malcolm and his friends tried to burn the place down, jus' before dawn," Mr. Tapley gasped, and the two men exclaimed in shock and disgust. "But President Houston sent us two of Captain Hays' rangers to help and we're all right."

The older man spat on the ground in disgust, while the younger added a few choice epithets, concluding with, "That no-count snake in the grass!" At that moment, Patrick Chevallier emerged from the house, and the older man chuckled.

"Another dissatisfied plaintiff, I see, Chevallier, but a luckier one than most of them as have met you at dawn. Well, we'll let all know what happened here."

"We're glad to see you, Lewison, and your boy as well," Patrick Chevallier answered. "Good neighbors are to be cherished, especially since ..." here, he cast a scornful glance at Hake Malcolm, "... the lawless and dissolute feel free to run roughshod over good citizens."

"Seh, we would welcome you for breakfast, since you took such trouble," Jubal spoke from beside Chevallier. "At least, some coffee an' some of Hebe's mighty fine beaten biscuits."

"Don't mind if I do," replied the older Lewison, tying up his horse team to a nearby railing. "Been so quiet 'round here of late, I rather relish a 'ruction of some kind – keeps me on my toes an' from getting old."

At that moment, another team appeared in the gravel drive. This was no ordinary farm wagon, but an elegant, closed carriage, drawn by a matched pair of teams, and driven by a liveried coachman; an odd equipage for Texas, but perhaps not quite so odd, for those portions which had long been settled.

"Who's this?" Jim whispered to Patrick Chevallier, whose' wary and tense countenance relaxed upon setting eyes on the man now springing with energy from the coach, even before the coach halted; a young-appearing man, with a weathered countenance and a forceful expression upon it. He strode toward the house; a man righteously wrathful and intent upon immediate answers, a man upon whom the dogs, Hera and Zeus immediately fawned, loping alongside and begging for caresses, while the household servants gathered, murmuring in amazement.

Mr. Lewison exclaimed, "Well, I'll be! Everyone thought he was lost, lost at sea!"

"He is our god from out of the machine," Patrick Chevallier replied, just as Jim recalled who this new man looked like. "Welcome home, at long last, Mr. Malcolm!"

"Patrick! Morris!" the young man reached the steps and came up them in a single bound, clasping hands first with Patrick Chevallier, then Mr. Tapley. "What in the name of all that's holy has been going on here? You said in your letter that there was a crisis brewing and I should return at once, but I never expected to find this mayhem! Who are these people, and what have they done?"

"Your cousin Hake," Patrick Chevallier indicated the groaning man on the improvised litter. "Took it on himself to claim Pecan Grove as his own, out of a noble sense of duty as your parents' sole living relation. He recruited a group of so-called friends, to whom he owed considerable sums, and they attempted to override your mother's last will and testament by attacking Pecan Grove and assassinating the primary legatee – your mother's pet macaw."

"That so?" Young Malcolm's expression hardened. "That cowardly, yellow-bellied, lying scum!" his eye fell upon his cousin, who in a moment of belated awareness, was struggling up from the improvised litter.

"I can explain, Jerimia…" he pleaded, before Young Malcolm reached down with both hands; knotted, powerful hands they were, from all those years at sea – and hauled his cousin to stand upright. One bunched fist held Hake Malcolm's dirty shirt-front and round jacket; the other fist struck a roundhouse blow that splattered blood from Hake's broken nose.

"No, you can't!" Snarled Young Malcolm. "Not to my satisfaction! You sponged off my father, calumniated my mother, shamed our family name in every way imaginable, and then you compounded your folly by attacking my home. Now, get out! And don't you dare show your face at Pecan Grove ever again!" And with that, he flung his cousin bodily off the verandah with such force that the latter fell headlong, landing at the feet of a very surprised young woman carrying an infant in one arm, and leading a small boy by the hand with the other, who had just been handed down from the carriage.

"Jedidiah, my dear – is this someone to whom I should be introduced?" she asked, in pleasant tones which hinted at her British origins.

"Only an unsatisfactory relation, and disgrace to the family name," Young Malcolm replied, resettling the collar of his coat. "And one who would be well-advised never to darken the doors of Pecan Grove again."

"Most families do have their black sheep," the young lady replied, with unruffled composure. Young Malcom set a reassuring arm around her.

"Theodora, my dear, let me introduce you to Mr. Patrick Chevallier, who acted for my parents in legal matters, and whom I hope will continue to do the same for us; Mr, Chevallier, this is my wife, Theodora. We married in Canton, where her father has considerable mercantile interests. Our son Josiah, and the baby Harriet. We've come home to Pecan Grove – and intend to stay!"

"That certainly resolves the matter of inheriting Pecan Grove," Jim observed to Patrick Chevallier and Toby, as they rode away the following morning. "The lost heir returned, with two of his own children! I'd say the future of Pecan Grove is secure for both Jedidiah Malcom and his namesake macaw."

"So, where had Mr. Malcolm been, all this time?" Toby had been ascertaining the safety of the slave quarters and Jedidiah the Macaw and had not been present when explanations for that long absence had been made.

"In Canton, China," Patrick Chevallier replied. "His ship was apparently broken apart in a violent storm, in which all the crew save himself drowned, or perished in the lifeboats. Only he survived, but injured and insensible, when rescued by a British ship on the way to Canton. He had lost all recollection of his identity. They presumed him to be American from his speech, and an educated man from his familiarity with poetry and literature; he wrote in a decent hand, so a charitable British merchant in Canton took pity and hired him as a bookkeeper. Eventually, he rose in the estimation of that merchant, was taken into partnership and married the merchant's daughter. A year or so ago, he began to recover his memories; small, inconsequential things at first. But when he recollected his name, and the existence of Pecan Grove, all became plain. It took a considerable time to send letters, and receive replies, from half the world away, and without any confirmation of his identity, I was skeptical and wished to wait until Mr. Malcolm arrived in Richmond, and to be recognized by those who had known him – hence my discretion. I did not want to aid an imposter or raise false hopes."

"In any case, I am certain that your client will do what he can for the plantation folk. Curses on the infernal peculiar institution of slavery!" Jim added, in sudden exasperation.

"It has been a constant throughout history," Patrick Chevallier pointed out. "In many places and practiced among many nations and peoples. Still – we can take comfort in the fact that many among us consider it an abomination and are working tirelessly for abolition of the vile practice."

"Still, I would see folk like Jubal and Jonas, and Persephone, Perlie and the little boys – to be free in their own lives." Jim noted, with regret.

"But they are, Brother," Toby spoke up unexpectedly. "As for your law – words on paper, only. In their hearts and minds, they are already free; free to act in their own interests, to take up weapons and defend their homes, their wives, and children. When your white law changes, and all men are free, it will mean little to those at Pecan Grove. They are already free."

2 – The Second Adventure: The King of Kibera

Wherein Jim and Toby guide a famous English adventurer into the Ironbelly Country ... with dire results!

"There's a pair of strangers in town, looking for Captain Jack," said the owner of the general store on the edge of the Plaza, "Foreigners, I think – English, by their talk. I reckon you'll do, Jim, if he ain't around."

"Captain Jack went to Austin to confab with General Houston," Jim replied, with a sigh. "Won't be back for another week or even longer. Did they say what they wanted?" Jim emptied a few coins and notes out of his purse in payment for a bag of green coffee beans, a larger bag of cornmeal, a small jar of molasses and a couple of sticks of sugar candy. He and Toby Shaw had just returned from an inquiry mission to Bastrop, resolving the matter of a missing girl, to an empty HQ and a note from their commander, informing Jim that meanwhile, he was in charge as Jack's senior stiletto-man in Bexar, and to manage matters for the Rangers as he thought best.

"Nope," the shopkeeper wiped his hands on the front of his apron and swept the coins off the countertop."

"Englishmen, hey?" Jim collected up the groceries into a small sack which had once contained wheat flour. "They didn't have an official look to them, did they?" He had a bad memory of an encounter with a duplicitous Englishman who claimed to be an actor not more than a year before. "What did they look like?"

"Born to the manor," the shopkeeper replied, "The taller one acted like a lord – flashy sort, with a fine-cut coat and an embroidered weskit. He did most of the talking."

"Did they say what they wanted?" Jim was in a hurry, but as this had the distinctive marks of a matter to which he should take note.

"Looking for a guide into the Ironbelly Canyon country, across the Pecos," the shop keep replied, "The tall Englishman said he has a mission there. Said he was going to leave his card at your place, hoped to speak with you at your earliest convenience. Didn't say anything more than that." Jim whistled in astonishment.

"That's some dangerous country," Jim said, over his shoulder. "The Kibera ain't no tribe anyone wants to mess with. As far as I know, there's been no white man visiting them since the Coronado expedition – what, two, three hundred years ago? I hope they've got their affairs in order, and a fine tombstone already paid for. Even the Comanche tread carefully in the Ironbelly."

* * *

"We've never been into the Ironbelly Country, have we?" Jim asked his blood-brother, Toby Shaw of the Delaware later that evening, as they ate a contented supper at twilight that evening, with the door to Captain Jack's headquarters house open to the slight evening breeze and the sound of music and distant voices from the Plaza Major drifting in. The music from the fandango hall just down the way was slightly louder than the bells of San Fernando cathedral. Madame Candelaria, the keeper of the fandango hall, was a particular friend of Captain Hays and those who worked as his stiletto-men among the Texas Rangers. She was a lady of certain years, indominable, bossy and known for her charitable works among the poor and sick – and also as a notable gossip. She had sent them a supper of half a roasted chicken, a dish of rice cooked with saffron, and a stack of paper-thin Mexican flat bread wrapped in a warmed towel. Madame Candelaria did this often, for she was quite fond of Captain Jack and his men and took a motherly attitude toward them all. She was certain in her own mind that they did not take care of themselves or eat good suppers, as they would if they had mothers or wives to see to them. In the absence of either, Madame nominated herself to oversee the welfare of a bachelor household.

"No, James – we have not," Toby replied. He sat cross-legged before the hearth, in which a small steeple of kindling sat, ready to be lit if the later evening chill called for a fire. "It is … a curious place."

A pair of calling cards sat on the table which doubled as a dining table and as a desk, where Jim was eating his own meal of chicken and rice.

"We had better come up to scratch on it, before our visitors present themselves," Jim observed, and fingered the pair of calling cards – thick, expensively-printed things, obviously of the best quality. *Alexander James Connaway, Bart.*, read the first. There was no address, only a short message on the reverse: *"We shall call upon you on the 7ᵗʰ inst, this day, to discuss a matter of some import."* The other card read The Honorable Richard Coign-Gordon, with a notation of Amesbury House. There was no annotation on that card. "Go ahead and tell me what you know of the tribe that lives there. It came to me this afternoon, as I was looking through the new additions to the lending library – if this Sir Alexander Connaway is the one with an account of his travels in Arabia, Mongolia, and Peru – than he is a noted explorer. He's looking for fresh fields to conquer – or at least, to scribble another volume of notable exploits."

"Ah, then," Toby wiped his lips with the last bite of his own flatbread, belched slightly and set aside his own empty plate. Madame Candelaria kept a fine kitchen. "The Kibera are a curious folk, James – they hold to themselves in the mesas of the Ironbelly Country. They are said to be silver mines there, and veins of turquoise stone, which the Kibera hold fast. They live in ancient houses of stone, many feet up from the valley floor, at the end of heavily defended pathways. They cultivate fields of corn and orchards of fruit on the mesa tops or in secure valleys watered by springs and streams. Few travelers venture there, and even fewer return," Toby added, with an oddly professorial air. "They keep to themselves, defend themselves most fiercely against their enemies – the Comanche, the Apache, even the Hopituh and the Dineh."

"A nut too hard to crack," Jim agreed.

Toby nodded, sagely. "They do not raid or trade; having given no offense or insult to any, they do not suffer insult in kind.

"What else do your folk know of the Kibera?" The bucket from the well of Jim's knowledge on this matter came up mostly empty. It seemed that Toby knew only a little more.

"Not much," Toby admitted. "They do say that they choose a king for themselves, much as white men do – crowned with silver and turquoise. That is why the Spaniard Coronado sent emissaries to the Ironbelly Country. The Spanish were mad for silver, and gold, too" Toby added, rather unnecessarily, as footsteps sounded in the street outside their door. Someone rapped upon the open door.

"Our visitors are early," Jim murmured, hastily cramming the last bit of his supper in his mouth. "A moment!" he called, and took his plate, spoon, and Toby's into the inner room. He straightened his coat, ran his fingers through his hair, went to the doorway and addressed the two men waiting outside. "Gentlemen, welcome to Bexar on behalf of Captain Hays. You mentioned that your interests lay in the Ironbelly Country. I do not know quite how we might assist you in this, as that lies somewhat outside our usual interests. I'm James Reade, Esquire, and this is my brother, Mr. Toby Shaw of the Delaware. Do come in; make yourselves at home, tell us what the nature of your business is in the Ironbelly Country."

"A pleasure!" enthused the taller and more elegant of the two gentlemen, pumping Jim's hand as if he hoped to bring water to the surface by his effort. He was tall, with bright blue eyes, a fresh complexion and broad shoulders which seemed to fill half the room. Unfashionably long fair hair fell past his shoulders, flowing unbound in the manner of a bold Saxon warrior of old. "A pleasure which is all mine, I assure you, Reade! Alexander Connaway here. My cousin, Coign-Gordon. The good man who referred me to your offices claimed that there is no better a one for knowledge of the wilderness! And it's the wilderness that beguiles us, Reade – enchants like a lovely siren, tempting us farther and farther on."

Jim, concealing a sigh of mild exasperation, showed Sir Alexander and his friend to the two most comfortable chairs in the room, while Toby took their coats, and Sir Alexander's elegant ebony and silver walking stick. "I am not certain how we might be of assistance to you," he ventured, once they were settled, and had exchanged some mild remarks regarding the weather, the allures of Bexar in the spring, and the relative beauty of the Texas countryside, which Sir Alexander and his cousin compared very favorably to England. Meanwhile, his companion, a slimmer and younger man with not half the presence of the English milord, favored Jim with a brief nod and a smile, and surprisingly – addressed Toby in a strange language, in tones which mingled curiosity and deep respect. Toby concealed his surprise well, at being addressed in his own tongue.

Finally, Sir Alexander set his hat – an elegant and fashionable beaver – on his knee and leaned forward. "I am certain that you will be able to assist us, sir!" He assured Jim with great confidence.

"Ah, but you can be of enormous help," Sir Alexander assured them both with quite touching earnest, "at least as far as the Ironbelly – and not so much as guides, for I daresay that Coign-Gordon and myself can blunder about and eventually make ourselves known to the Kibera, but it would save time and patience to have an introduction to this country of yours from one said to be knowledgeable. Even though I spent months in the archives of the Spanish crown in Madrid, you still possess a well of knowledge, from which we both must drink deep... surely you can see your way to be our guide, for at least part of our journey. I would not insult you by offering you mere money," Sir Alexander fixed Jim with a gaze of profound respect and Jim felt himself beginning to yield; for the Englishman was powerfully persuasive. It also would be to the interest of Texas in the current political climate, to have been helpful to a man of no small influence in England.

With a glance at Toby, who perceived his thoughts and assented with a tiny nod of his own head, Jim replied, "Of course we shall be glad to guide you, as far as the edge of Texas' claimed territory, as that is our charge and responsibility – but to the edge of the Ironbelly."

"Capital!" Sir Alexander enthused. "When shall we set out then, gentlemen? Pray, let us not delay for I have been planning this expedition for many months. I have procured several good riding horses and a pair of pack mules for ourselves ... I do not travel with any greater train, Mr. Reade; the larger the party, the greater the difficulty and the slower progress, and the greater the chance of inadvertently offending the genii of the place!"

"Very sensible of you," Jim agreed, somewhat cheered to find that the noble adventurer was not about to stand on ceremony, and in fact, seemed to be a most sensible and agreeable man. "And I agree with you, as regards a small party. We will be happy to serve as your guide, but my brother and I must take a day or so to arrange our own affairs, then – say in four days?"

"Splendid!" Sir Alexander beamed with the frank enthusiasm of a small child promised a treat. "Most splendid. Thank you for your consideration, sirrah. At this place at first light, in four days! We shall see you then."

The two Englishmen took their courteous leave, after Sir Alexander thanked Jim yet again for his assistance. Jim saw them to the front door, and closed it after them, after being assured yet again of their gratitude and willingness to embark on their expedition in four days. There was a long silence in the room, finally broken when Jim ventured,

"Well?"

"Most interesting, James," Toby replied. He was busying himself with lighting the fire, and his back was turned toward Jim, so he could not see his friend's expression. "And most curious. The milord's cousin – a man who searches out and hunts down languages as if they were rare toys. As if it were a sport. He spoke the language of my people very well, although with a strange accent. I wonder ..." he hesitated for a moment, and Jim looked searchingly at his blood-brother.

"Wonder what?"

"What it really is that the milord wants," Toby blew upon the wavering flame, which he had coaxed to light with a patent lucifer match. "I cannot see what that might be, James – and that worries me."

Jim threw himself into the comfortable chair which Sir Alexander had so lately occupied. "Adventure ... the plaudits of his friends in England, the learned members of the Royal Geographical Society, and the attention of pretty ladies. To travel strange new lands, encounter new and wilder people than any of his peers have done ..."

"You like him, do you not, James?"

"He was most satisfactory company," Jim admitted. "Original, erudite, well-traveled. Yes, I do like him, and there are a great many men whom I have liked rather less. What did you think of his cousin, the Honorable Coign-Gordon? You spoke long with him, and I did not – what manner of man did you judge him to be?"

Toby looked thoughtfully into the fire, twisting yellow and blue flames dancing above the dried mesquite and sage. Their scent was pleasantly aromatic in the small room.

"A purer ambition than his cousin, but he is the ... not the weaker of the of the two ... the less determined, I think. He will follow wherever the milord leads. Born to be a companion, by which I do not mean a lesser man. But one content to be the sworn spear-companion, rather than the war-leader."

"I think that after conveying them as far as the Ironbelly," Jim considered it all, and stifled a yawn. "We might very well know exactly what motivates Sir Alexander and the Honorable Coign-Gordon. At any rate, Captain Jack will approve that we have been making such influential friends on behalf of the nation."

The journey west to the Ironbelly Country – an arid land of towering flat-topped mesas and rock formations, threaded with tiny streams – progressed much as the initial evening had done; companionable and relatively uneventful. They were blessed by mild spring weather, and only a little inconvenienced by occasional rain. The 'milord', Sir Alexander, and the Honorable Coign-Gordon, proved to be as amiable and adept traveling companions in the unsettled, Comanche-haunted country to the west of Bexar as they had been good company on the occasion of their initial visit. Both had forsworn their fine coats and elegant accoutrements for plain linen, sturdy trousers, and hard-wearing leather hunting coats suitable for the frontier. The gear and supplies they brought with them – secured in packs born by a pair of well-behaved miles – were of good make, well-worn through use, and excellent in quality. Richard Coign-Gordon had navigational instruments and took a sighting through the marine sextant every day at noon as they journeyed. The younger man also kept copious notes, illustrated with many painstaking sketches of items of interest, large and small. It was indeed a most scientific expedition.

To Jim's mild astonishment, Sir Alexander carried as his single personal weapon, a powerful recurve bow of wood and horn and a supply of short iron-tipped arrows together in a long leather case of peculiar design slung over his shoulder, rather than a firearm.

"It's a Scythian bow," he explained when Jim remarked upon it. "Made to the ancient pattern – I took to that form of archery the expedition to Uhlan-Baator – practiced at it, ever since. Jolly good fun, too – much quieter than a pistol. Sometimes the old ways are better than our newfangled notions, eh?"

He was also given to sing, in an energetic baritone; his favorite melody was *The Minstrel Boy*.

Meadows of lush grass, starred with wildflowers – pink, blue and yellow – spread out before them as if on a canvas splashed by a cosmic artist with a mad paintbrush. Within a week of travel, they had gone beyond the cultivated fields and the pastures tended by shepherds with their flocks of sheep and goats, far beyond the herds of wild cattle and horses, and into the hunting grounds haunted by the wandering Comanche. Some days after they crossed the Buckhorn Draw, they overtook a small party of Penateka on the trail and moving with purpose – a hunting party, to Jim's relief.

"They have women with them," he explained in an undertone to Sir Alexander and Richard, as Toby rode ahead of their horses, and the pair of laden pack mules. "See … there, with the loose horses. If it were a war party, then there would be no women. Which is to our good fortune. And these are Penateka, with whom Mr. Shaw and I are friends, thanks to the good word of their wise old medicine man, Mopechucope, the Old Owl."

"I knew that your guidance companionship would be an excellent thing," Sir Alexander replied, with great good humor. They sat on their horses and watched Toby conferring with the leader of the party. Richard Coign-Gordon watched the proceedings with great intensity, plainly seeing yet another tongue for his linguistic collection within his grasp.

The wind rustled the tall grass at their feet, grass already almost belly-high to their horses and mules, a frieze of pale russet grass-heads crowning the green waves. After several minutes of converse, Toby nodded cordially to the leader of the Comanche party and returned to join the others.

"As we thought, Jim," he said. "They are hunting. They are curious about our friends – I have said that they are well-traveled and very wise men, with tales of many lands and peoples. They have invited us to join the hunting party tomorrow – a feast of fat cow, they say. Are you interested, milord – in joining the Comanche tomorrow at first light?"

"I would be delighted," Sir Alexander beamed with suppressed excitement. "Mr. Shaw, if you would be so kind as to convey my agreement to ... er ... the gentlemen of the Comanche."

"You should be warned," Jim explained, as Toby went to tell the hunting party of their noble guest. "They hunt buffalo with a spear – it's the manly thing."

"How splendid!" Sir Alexander beamed again. "What an experience! Like pig-sticking! – with a two-thousand-pound pig!"

Jim sighed – the man's enthusiasm knew no limits. He hoped that Sir Alexander's luck knew no limits, either.

That evening, they camped in some amity with the hunting party, and shared the evening meal – Toby and Richard Coign-Gordon's heads together as Toby parsed out some of the Comanche's vocabulary for the edification of the linguistic collector. The male hunters admired Sir Alexander's exotic bow and marveled at his speed and accuracy when he demonstrated his facility with it – a skill nearly the equal of the Comanche themselves. It didn't escape Jim's notice also that the three young Comanche women with the hunters admired Sir Alexander's person with no less appreciation.

The hunt went well, although Jim did not see it; merely the fine results afterwards. He and Toby broke camp and followed the hunting party's trail the next morning at midday. They overtook the two Englishmen at the scene of the successful hunt; a dozen half-butchered buffalo scattered on the trampled grass, bloody viscera heaped here and there, already masked by a seething mass of hungry flies. The women had the great shaggy hides pegged out, scraped skin up and already drying in the sun, and strips of Morocco-leather colored buffalo flesh drying on peeled willow twig racks over a smoky fire. There were also fresh cuts of buffalo flesh sizzing over the fire, the men of the hunting party taking their leisure around it with the air of men whose' job was satisfactorily accomplished. The delectable odor of roasting meats hung on the air, and Jim's mouth couldn't help but water. Sir Alexander rode up to the party, beaming.

"'Straordinary!" He exclaimed. "It was most 'straordinary, Mr. Reade! Cut out the beast, match stride and thrust away! What an exhilarating experience! And by-the-by, I have our supper tonight! A whole tender cut of the best part of the buffalo – the Queen herself couldn't dine on anything more luscious than this!"

Sir Alexander's enthusiasm couldn't be more engaging, or infectious; Jim was glad of that – and that the noble

Englishman and his mount had taken no more harm to themselves but a cut from an enraged buffalo's horn to the horses' flank. Toby doctored the creature himself with a poultice of salt and some medicinal herbs produced from a small store in his saddlebags. Toby put much stock in his medicinal herbs and having been successfully doctored with them on their first meeting, Jim did as well.

Their small party moved on, taking a courteous farewell of the Comanche party – who being glutted and content with their takings, barely roused themselves to bid farewell, although Jim did note that the three Comanche women appeared somewhat downcast as they rode away. Later that afternoon, as the sun began to slide down into the west and cast long blue shadows across the land, Sir Alexander spurred his horse ahead, so that he and Jim could consult about where to camp for the night.

"Mr. Shaw has seen the swifts flying low, with mud in their beaks," Jim said, "Which means water, somewhere ahead. It's mostly dry country ahead, so we should make the most of water when we find it."

"Very good," Sir Alexander agreed. "I say, Reade – how many more days until we reach the Ironbelly, do you think?"

"About another day, if all goes well," Jim replied."

"And then we shall part our ways," Sir Alexander shaded his eyes against the lowering sun and peered ahead. "With regret, I must admit – but since your remit only goes as far as the Ironbelly. I say, I have meant to ask; did you ever wonder why it is called the Ironbelly Country?"

"Most men think that it is called so because it is hot as an iron skillet heated over a fire." Jim replied. "But the explanation that I believe was given once by Colonel James Bowie and some friends, who went with a party exploring this part of the country in '31, some years before he fell in battle at the Alamo. They were prospecting for horses and silver, and came this way, knowing that the Spanish expedition under Coronado might also have passed by. And so they had. There was, Colonel Bowie reported, the skeleton of a man in Spanish armor – breastplate, helmet and greaves. It appeared very much as if he had been buried in haste centuries before at the edge of a dry watercourse, and later the very land weathered away, revealing the bones and armor. Shortly after this discovery, they were warned by their Lipan Apache guide that they should venture no further, because they were on the edge of Kibera lands. Colonel Bowie was disappointed in not finding the legendary silver mines, but as they were running short of supplies, they decided to return, discretion being the better part of valor."

"A skeleton in armor!" Sir Alexander exclaimed, "My dear Reade, how quite terribly gothic! And here Coign and I thought that Texas was such a mundane, modern place. Ah well, such is the power of illusion. I should confess to you before we part. I have an ambition, a quite overwhelming one."

"And that is?" Jim ventured, more in an idle manner to keep the conversation going. Sir Alexander was erudite, amusing, insightful, a breath of fresh intellectual air and a visitor from a wider world. "Something to do with the Ironbelly Country and the Kibera folk?"

"Why yes, indeed," Sir Alexander favored Jim with a blindingly confident smile. "I intend to become their king."

"You ... what?" Jim stared at him, utterly boggled, while their horses plodded onward. "Their king? But the tribes in the west – as far as I know – do not have kings. More the pity, for such might form a reliable and authoritative government, with which we might deal to our mutual benefit. Instead ... their small divisions do as they wish, making war or peace as the mood takes them... become their king, Sir Alexander?"

"Indeed," Sir Alexander repeated patiently. "I know – a mad ambition, you might think. But I have done the research, in the archives in Spain. The Kibera indeed have a king – a god-king, sent by the almighty feathered serpent as his emissary on earth! So I intend to become theirs. Crowned with silver, dusted with gold, and washed in the waters of the sacred spring at the heart of Kibera. Think of what I might be able to accomplish, Richard and I together!"

"That ... would be an interesting development," was all that Jim could bring himself to admit, after punching down his initial sentiment – that Sir Alexander had gone as mad as any in Bedlam. King of the Kibera? On the far frontier, king of a tribe which had kept isolated since before Coronado, keeping themselves to themselves? "Do you believe that it can be successfully accomplished?"

"Certainly," Sir Alexander replied, with such confidence that Jim felt his heart sinking. The man meant it, every word. "I have studied every record of every encounter of the Spanish with the Kibera. Mr. Reade, there were reports from Spanish missionaries which never were published. They are a sophisticated folk – superstitious when it comes to their gods – but I have every confidence."

"You are betting your life on this," Jim warned him, and Sir Alexander laughed.

"What is life but a long series of gambles, Mr. Reade! The higher the stakes, the sweeter the success! And I am a man accustomed to winning my gambles. Do you know – when I am King of Kibera, I will send emissaries to Her Majesty, Victoria, proposing an alliance. Your Texas will have a close ally in me, of course – an alliance such as your President Houston has been proposing."

"I am certain that President Houston will be in favor of such a relationship," Jim finally brought himself to say, in as tactful a way as he could. "I cannot speak for him, of course ... but I can guarantee that such treaties as you suggest would be carefully considered by those higher in the administration than I am."

"Excellent!" Sir Alexander beamed approval. "Ah – I see that Mr. Shaw is approaching! I take it that he has located a fine camp for us. We will dine on fresh buffalo tonight; Richard tells me that our Comanche friends assured me that our share of my kill today is of the most succulent ..."

The noble Englishman continued talking, of other and inconsequential matters. Jim listened with half an ear, racking his mind for some notion of how to discourage Sir Alexander from the insane course of action which he seemed determined to embark upon. In the end he concluded that there really was nothing he could do, save at the last minute of their parting the following day, at the edge of a wide dry riverbed, snaking it's way across the arid landscape, already shimmering with heat-devils rising under the mid-morning sun.

"Well, here is where we must part," Sir Alexander leaned from his saddle to shake Jim's hand. "Thank you and Mr. Shaw for your guidance – the next time we meet, you must make a bow to royalty, you know."

"I'm a man of Texas," Jim returned sturdily. "We bow only to the Almighty. I wish that I might discourage you from this course, Sir. Alexander. It is perilous in the extreme, and ..."

"Stuff and nonsense!" Sir Alexander replied, merrily. "No, we will not be dissuaded from this venture. Richard and I have sworn solemn oaths on the matter; that I will be the King of Kibera and he will be my First Minister! And so farewell, Mr. Reade, Mr. Shaw!"

With a whoop and a clatter of hooves on the stones at their feet, the two Englishmen spurred their horses, the pair of pack mules following after with marked reluctance as was the way of mules. Jim and Toby sat on their own horses, watching Sir Alexander's small party diminish in the distance, the brooding mesa in the distance topped by a towering white cloud which threatened rain by afternoon. The words of Sir Alexander's favorite song floated back to them, muted by distance. *"The minstrel boy to the war has gone, in the ranks of death you will find him! His father's sword he has girded on, and his wild harp slung behind him..."*

Jim hoped sincerely that those lines were not prophetic.

"You couldn't convince him to abandon this venture, my brother?" Toby said at last. "To be the king of the Kibera folk?"

Jim shook his head. "No. I could not. He would not hear of anything to dissuade him. Which I regret ... as I fear that he goes to his death."

"All men die, my brother," Toby replied. "The fortunate have the choosing of the manner and the moment in which they meet Death. And perhaps ..."

"Perhaps, what?"

Toby laughed and reined his horse around, to the east and the trail which led back to Bexar. "Perhaps the milord might become a king after all – in the end, only the Great Sky Father knows what is written for a man's fate!"

    * * *

In Bexar, Jack was waiting for them, the afternoon that Jim and Toby returned, covered with trail-dust and mildly depressed that they had not been able to persuade the two Englishmen aside from the reckless course which they had set upon. Jack looked up from the table where he had inkwell and paper laid out, a report half-written before him.

"There you are," he remarked. "Anything interesting happen while I was in Austin? Madame Candelaria said that you and gone to lead a pair of Englishmen into the Ironbelly Country; the explorer Sir Alexander Connaway and his cousin, Richard Coign-Gordon."

"We did," Jim replied. "We departed from them, at their request at the edge of the Ironbelly. Sir Alexander says that he is determined to become the King of the Kibera."

"Ah," Jack dipped his pen into the ink and made another line to his report, utterly nonplussed. The pen made a faint scratching sound on the coarse paper. "So ... merely another ordinary mission for my stiletto-men, eh?"

"That was the long and short of it," Jim agreed, and Toby chuckled.

* * *

And that was the last mention, or sight of Sir Alexander and the Honorable Richard for a very long time. Other missions and emergencies took the attention of Jack Hays and his stiletto-men. In time the matter of the prospective King of Kibera faded into the dimmest of recollections. Until the day – a rainy autumn afternoon – when a long Santa Fe freight wagon pulled by eight yoke of oxen rolled slowly into the Plaza Mayor and splashed to a halt before the house which served as home and headquarters for Captain Hays. Rain drummed on the canvas cover and sluiced into the trampled mud of the plaza. A fringe of rain poured in regular streams from the edge of the tiled roof. The window shutters and the heavy oak door stood open in the thick adobe walls, left open to admit the cooler air.

"'sis the place where Capn' Jack Hays might be found?" the teamster rapped on the door frame, as rain dripped from his hat and soaked the heavy woolen serape draped around his shoulders. "We had a passel o' freight to bring to Bexar.

They tol' me I ought to bring the crazy man here. We found him wandering along the trail near the Canadian crossing. He's sick and crippled up some."

"Crazy man?" Jack looked out into the gray veil of rain, which had doubled down in intensity, even as thunder grumbled overhead. "This is my office, not an asylum for the insane."

"Wal," the teamster scratched his bristly cheek. "Fac' is, the crazy man hisself ast to come here. Says he is pals with Mr. Reade ... him an' Shaw the Indian led him to the Ironbelly Country, almost two years ago it was, so he says."

"Tell him to come in, then," Jack said, and added as an aside. "Well ... if'n he is that sick, I'll go around to Madame Candelaria. She's the best nurse of sick folk that I know, bless her. If that's one of your old English pals, he doesn't look real well, at all."

For a ragged, stooped, and bare-legged creature, barely recognizable as a human being was now descending from the wagon and shambling toward the doorway.

"He's all your'n," observed the teamster, and squelched his way back to his team. With a crack of his great whip – somewhat dampened by the incessant rain, the wagon creaked away. Meanwhile, Jim – remembering some of his mother's remedies for the sick and soaked to the bone – went into the inner room and brought out a dry blanket and his own pair of woolen slippers. Toby, unbidden, set the smallest of their pots closest to the hearth to warm the water and a sprinkling of his medicinal herbs within, and added more dry wood to the fire.

"This is unlooked for, Brother," he murmured. "Is it the milord, or his kinsman, the collector of words?"

"I don't know," Jim replied, appalled at the wreck of a man, the sheer misery reflected in the bent posture and shambling gait of the man approaching the door. He was wrapped in what looked like a blanket, a very ragged, threadbare, and filthy blanket. Crude moccasins covered in mud covered his feet. A turban of dirty, soaked cloth veiled the man's head. Otherwise, Jim was certain that he would recognize Sir Alexander's Saxon-fair mane, and his breadth of shoulder. The only man it could be was Richard Coign-Gordon, bent over a small bundle wrapped in an old flour-sack which he held in his arms. What had happened, in the years when he and Toby had bidden goodbye to the dauntless explorer. One thing was certain. Sir Alexander hadn't been anointed and crowned as the king of the Kibera. The tale of why and how that quest had failed was about to be revealed to them all. Jack Hays murmured,

"Look after him, boys. Me, I'm going to alert Madame Candelaria that she has a new patient. He looks in a bad way

"Coign-Gordon, is it you?" Jim asked, gently, as the man hesitated at the door. "Come in and sit down, rest yourself by the fire. You do not look well – you must have undergone many hardships in your journey."

"They were kind, the drovers were..." Richard Coign-Gordon mumbled. His teeth clattered together as he shivered violently. "A rough lot, but kind. Very kind." The young Englishman was just barely recognizable; his face seamed and scarred, especially about the eyes, as if he had aged twenty years, instead of only two. His hands, clutching the bundle to his chest, were also scarred, almost claw-like. He tottered toward the most comfortable chair, set before the tiny fire

"Let me take that ..." Jim made as if to relieve Coign-Gordon of the bundle, but with a flare of alarm in his eyes, the man clutched it to him.

"No, no ... it's his!"

The reaction was so hysterical that Jim desisted. Instead, he said, "Your outer garment is wet, and your shoes, too ... let me take them to dry by the fire. You'll catch your death of cold, with your feet wet and cold. That's what my mother always says."

Richard Coign-Gordon laughed, a croaking, gasping laugh which ended in a racking cough. He did permit Jim to take the blanket from around his shoulders, and the soaked moccasins from his feet. Silently, Toby knelt and replaced them with slippers, while Jim wrapped the dry blanket around his shoulders.

"Now tell us what happened, when you and Sir Alexander met with the Kibera ... you did meet with them, didn't you? Your cousin was set on it, set on becoming their king, and you as his First Minister."

"They crucified me," Richard Coign-Gordon gasped, when he could speak again. "And I had never done anyone harm at all. Between two trees at the edge of the cliff they did it, so that I might watch. Cut my eyelids, too – so that I had to see what was done to Alexander. They thought I must die of it, but I didn't, and so they let me go the following day..."

"What happened," Jim had expected the matter of Sir Alexander's claim of kingship to go badly, but it sounded like the noble explorer's end had been gruesome far beyond Jim's expectations. "We left you at the edge of the Kibera lands almost two years ago – tell us what happened from the beginning. Did they accept Sir Alexander as their king?"

"He had a crown and all," Richard Coign-Gordon replied, and began to cough again. When the fit was past, he lay back against the chair. "He wears a crown! A king, and a most magnificent one. He strode among them like the god which most believed him to be."

"How did it start, then," Jim urged him. "Tell us ... you found the Kibera, I trust – and found a welcome from them."

"So we did," Coign-Gordon accepted the tin cup of herbal tea from Toby, wrapping his crippled, twisted fingers around it, as if he craved the warmth. "It was two, three days after we parted from you, on the edge of the Kibera lands. We rode into the largest of the canyons where their cliff-houses clung to the canyon walls like swift's nests, halfway between earth and Heaven. No one approached us until the second day, when a native appeared as we rode. He was an old man, but he wore a tunic of fine-woven fabric, worked with many beads and embroidery. He held out his empty hands, as if to say that he meant no harm. I spoke to him in the Delaware tongue ... and eventually we were made to understand that he was an emissary from the Kibera. They were curious to know our purpose, you see, having watched us for some days..." Coign-Gordon was wracked by another fit of coughing. When it eased. He continued the account of Sir Alexander's quest to become a king.

It seemed that Sir Alexander initially had impressed the Kibera. The old man, who first encountered them was called Kiahel, or Old Crow. He was a senior and influential wise man among the Kibera; a seer and medicine man who became Sir Alexander's champion. Jim was not surprised. The man had a magnetic character, and his self-assurance, and facility with words and weapons like his treasured Scythian bow.

"Kiahel was convinced that Alexander was indeed the beloved of the feathered serpent-god and sent by the divine to live and rule amongst the Kibera. With the good word of Kiahel he was accepted by their council of elders and proven warriors. Such simple folk we thought them! With much rejoicing, we were taken to the place that they called the House of the King, in the largest of their towns. The town was called Walato." Coign-Gordon began to cough again. Jim and Toby waited with some impatience for him to recover his voice. "A dizzy climb it was, up a path scarcely the width of three spans if that. And steep climbs up through foot and hand-holds pecked out from rock, or ladders, a dizzying height above the canyon floor. I was ill from the effort of not looking down! Heights ... I am not agreeable to them, gentlemen. The terrible fate of my cousin has done nothing, nothing, to cure me of such an aversion. But at first ... the chambers we were conducted into were very pleasant. A suite of rooms in the highest part of Walato. And there we were brought food, and drink, while Kiahel conferred with the chief men and warriors."

"Was Sir Alexander declared king right away?" Jim asked, and Coign-Gordon shook his head.

"No, it was many weeks, while the Kibera war chiefs and wise men from other villages came to confer. They had many questions and tests for him – tests of physical prowess and endurance, mostly. Marksmanship with his Scythian bow; for power and distance it surpassed their own bows. This astounded the Kibera warriors very much, for they have a great need of defensive weapons such as bows which could shoot an arrow twice as far and accurately as their own. Kiahel's oldest son was one of their war-leaders, a chief of the Eagle Society. A clever man, indeed; Alexander and I both began to think most highly of him, although our high opinions were eventually crushed. Treachery! Treachery and disloyalty! Kiahel's son urged his warriors to copy the Scythian bow, which they did with Alexander leading them against a raiding party of their enemies on one of the outlying villages. A successful defense ... In the end, the Kibera great council agreed that my cousin should be their king. The coronation was a strange and barbaric affair ..." Coign-Gordon was wracked with another fit of coughing. "... but ceremonial, in the fashion of a primitive people." Jim noticed his blood-brother's lips pressing tightly together, at that observation, although Toby made no comment.

One of their fellow stiletto-men, Bob Neighbors would later remark, "Think the Indians can't tell right from wrong? Wrong them and see what happens then!"

"They revere snakes – since their god appears everywhere in the form of a serpent. The king's crown is in the likeness of a silver serpent, set with turquoise. As part of the ceremony, they anointed him with a powder of ground maize and gold dust," Richard Coign-Gordon conquered another fit of coughing, and continued with the story. "Head to foot. We were given to understand that this ceremony was a yearly ritual; once anointed, the king was escorted to the sacred spring, in the heart of Kibera, where he must wash the dust from his body ... it was a desolate place, I tell you; a rock-lined pool, deep and cold ... haunted by scorpions and rattlesnakes, as are all seeps and springs in the desert... but their custom commanded."

"What happened then?" Jim urged him to continued, as Coign-Gordon's mind appeared to be wandering again. It was some moments before Coign-Gordon continued the tale.

"It went well, as well as we had hoped," the sick man clutched the bundle to his chest as if it were something dear and precious. "For a year, Alexander ruled like a god-king, in the sky-castle of Walato. I learned their language, of course, and shared many an evening of most jolly conversation. I also shared that knowledge of the tongue with him. Alexander led the parties which defended Kibera, consulted with the council of their wise elders. Success was in our grasp, complete success; Alexander had notions of marrying well among the important clans. We had no expectation of the disaster that would strike on the anniversary of his coronation, when the ritual of the maize and gold dust, the washing in the sacred spring was to be repeated."

"Disaster?" Jim prodded gently, as carefully as if he were examining a sympathetic but hostile-to-his case witness before a jury.

"It came without warning – the catastrophe," Coign-Gordon clutched the bundle to his chest, and to Jim's horror, began to weep. "Escorted by all the senior wise men, and the elder warriors – Alexander went to the spring, on the dawn of the day appointed. He strode forward, godlike, like Ajax ... and as he stepped out of the pool, a coiled snake struck, struck and sent its' fangs into his shin."

"An omen, a bad omen," Toby breathed. "For snakes are the embodiment of their god, the feathered serpent."

Coign-Gordon began to tremble, and his voice went shrill. "It all went bad, at that point. For everyone saw, saw and instantly believed that their serpent-god had spoken, and the king was a false one. They set about Alexander and I, laid violent hands upon us – I, who had been their friend, Alexander, who was their king! And they dragged us both, all protesting to the highest cliff above Walato. There they nailed my hands to a pair of trees, cut my eyelids so that I must watch – and they made him jump from that crag! They pointed spears at him – and he set the crown firmly upon his head and he leaped from that cliff and fell to the bottom, to the canyon below ... fell so far! Fell so far that it seemed to take hours... He shouted at them before he leapt from the cliff that they were a false people and worthy of punishment from their serpent-god for rejecting their true king ... and then he fell, fell so far!" That last ended on a sob, which turned into another violent coughing fit, just as Jack came through the

74

door with Madame Candelaria on his heels, and two boys from her household in her wake. When the fit passed, Coign-Gordon pressed his trembling, broken hands to his chest. "I expect they thought I would die ... but the next morning, when Kiahel and his son saw that I still lived – they pulled the spikes from my hands, took me down by secret paths to the foot of the cliffs and let me go free ... And all the time, Alexander led me, led me by the hand and never failed. I never let go of him ... and here I am. I have urgent business in the south and must see to it..." The feverish rambling died away in a mutter. Coign-Gordon appeared to have lapsed into a barely conscious state. Madame Candelaria took one look at him and exclaimed as she crossed herself in the old manner,

"*Dios mía* ... what did they do to him, *pobrecito!* Never mind – he is a child of God, so I shall take care, every care, as if he is one of my own blood!"

"Thank you, Madame," Jack replied. "He has suffered much, and we have no notion of how to care for someone so broken down by misfortune and torture!"

"Men!" sniffed Madame Candelaria, but it was merely a demonstration of pity for poor men who were incapable of managing a sick room or a small baby. "Diego, Mateo ... carry this poor fellow to the place in my home reserved for the sick; carefully, lest he awaken. Oh, what a fever he has!" she added, after brushing Coign-Gordon's forehead with her wrist. "But he is in my care now. With the help of the Lord, and Saint Jude, of those unknown causes of illness, he will recover, if it is willed so."

Barely conscious, Coign-Gordon was carried away bundled in Madame Candelaria's blankets by the two boys, the rain having let up for a few minutes. Jim thought that he was trying to speak – but it was only a whisper, the song that Sir Alexander would sing, *The Minstrel Boy*. Jim shivered, momentarily unsettled.

"I'll bring his boots and that bundle of his to Madame's tomorrow, when the rain lets up," Jim turned to his commander. "I'm sorry to hear his tale, Jack. I wish now that I had been able to talk Sir Alexander out of that mad notion of his."

"No, my brother," Toby shook his head. "It was his fate, and he went to it with open eyes, knowing the price of failure."

"Pity it took his pal with him," Jack settled into his chair and took out his pipe. "The world is full of folk whom you think would have known better than to dash headlong into peril which they could better have avoided. See if there is anything in that bundle of his which might have the whereabouts of his kinfolk. I suppose that I should write and let them know that their wandering lad has turned up in civilization and he's in a bad way."

Jim picked up the flour-sack bundle; the sole thing which Richard Coign-Gordon had carried away from the Ironbelly, and Sir Alexander's reign as king of the Kibera. Handling the sack, it felt as if there was only one object in it, something relatively hard and almost spherical. Jim opened the mouth of the sack and held it over the table.

The object within rolled out – a flash of a tarnished silver circlet in the shape of a snake set with turquoise, and dry blond hair, as dry as straw, adorning leathery dry flesh and an eyeless gaze from skeletal sockets. Jim, Jack, and Toby regarded it with horror, as it settled on the table. Still recognizable as the visage of Sir Alexander Connaway ... the erstwhile King of Kibera.

Finally, Jack cleared his throat. "Well ... we never had much truck with kings and all here in Texas and in the Ironbelly Country. I guess this is how his story ends."

3 – The Third Adventure: The Haunting of Bell House

Wherein Jim and Toby return to Galveston to investigate the matter of a haunted mansion.

"I have a curious errand for you," Jack laid down the most recent copy of the *Telegraph & Register*. "There is a most curious ruction going on even as we speak. In Galveston, which is your home range, Jim. Perhaps you might be able to call on the help of your father and his new law partner."

"A curious ruction?" Jim inquired. "Is it a matter of law? And I might mention, Jack – that all our errands from this department are curious. Some more curious than others, but all curious to some degree or other."

"Perhaps," Jack replied, with a wry smile of acknowledgment, "Perhaps this is one more on the extremely curious side of the scale. It might also be a matter for a man of the cloth, as a haunting is involved ... a good Catholic, like Father Odin, to perform an exorcism to drive out evil spirits. Or one of your Delaware medicine-workers, adept at chasing away a malign influence, with bells, smells and what-have-you."

"A dwelling haunted by a bad spirit, then?" Toby looked very grave. They were sitting all together in the front room of the tiny old-fashioned adobe house which served as Jack Hay's command headquarters in San Antonio – an old house built in the ancient Spanish fashion, of thick walls, low ceilings, and small shuttered windows; a house of plastered adobe and a sagging tile roof, which opened directly onto the main plaza of the old town. The weather was temperate, and they had propped the heavy door open, for the fresh air and wandering breeze which it admitted.

"In essence, that," Jack admitted. "But considerably more than a simple dwelling, my Delaware stiletto-man. It's a whole and entire mansion, the Bell mansion. A large house, located on a salubrious location on Galveston Island. It has been for sale by the nephews of the original owner ... only no one wishes to tender an offer to purchase, on the grounds that it is haunted. The few serious offers of purchase have been withdrawn ... with curious haste by those tendering them. A man of suspicious nature might detect the scent of a rat or something equally unsavory."

"There's more, Captain, I am certain," Jim replied. He was accustomed to Jack keeping back the interesting bits to their assignments; mostly because Jack had a perverse sense of humor. It appeared to amuse their commander no end, saving the twist for last. "It's an attractive house with a lovely garden. I recall it very well, since it was constructed in the last decade, on a scenic bit of property, and there should not be a problem in finding a buyer for it ... so what is the matter of concern to the Texas Rangers?"

"Well ... first because the heirs who want to sell have the ear of Jeptha Roberts, and one of the brothers is an intimate of President Lamar, and naturally ..." here Jack sighed, deep and heartfelt. "The concerns of our chief executive tend to become my concern. Passing strange how that works out, gentlemen!"

"Stuff rolls downhill," Jim noted, with cynicism. Jack nodded, wearily.

"Still, there is a smell to this matter which the brothers do not like. They are both of of the opinion that someone is deliberately putting about the tales of huge black dogs with fiery eyes, haunting their uncle's old home at midnight. Also – tales of strange lights and noises when the property is supposed to be vacant. What if this becomes a commonplace strategy, when it comes to the sale of a significant estate? All that someone need do who wishes to purchase for pennies on the dollar is to put about a story about a haunting, or some other unfortunate aspect..."

"I do not think potential buyers of so substantial a property would be sufficiently gullible to believe such tales," Jim began, and then realized that yes, he had observed many men whom he had thought intelligent and insightful, fall for the most transparent bits of fakery and delusion. "Is there something about the Bell mansion that makes such a tale credible?"

"Well, it seems that the Bell House was built over part of the foundations of Jean Lafitte's Campeachey pirate camp," Jack sat back with his pipe and looked meditatively into the fireplace, where in the colder months, a small fire of aromatic mesquite wood was accustomed to burn. As it was now summer, there was no need of a fire. Jack and his stiletto-men – whichever of them was at liberty and hanging about Jack's headquarters between missions – were accustomed to dining on red-bean stew purchased from the Mexican ladies who offered it by the bowl to all and sundry, or to partake of a generous and tasty meal send by Madame Candelaria, who had a motherly affection for Jack Hays and all those single young men who had employment with him on behalf of the well-being of the nation of Texas. She and her husband kept a dance hall, just off the Plaza Mayor; she was a well-known and charitable citizen, whose patriotism and sense of civic responsibility was without peer and above reproach.

"Ah ... that might explain it," Jim replied. "The Pirate Lafitte was supposed to have left caches of gold, silver and gems buried everywhere, hither and yon. My brother Dan and I ... as boys, we went searching over Campeachey for some of it. There were still some ruins and pits, and legends a plenty, and this was way before Bell built his mansion, which he never really got to enjoy, having died in a fit of apoplexy before it was ever finished. We never found a dratted thing – only a few British silver sixpences in the spoil at the front of some animal burrow, and my father gave us both a good talking-to, over trespassing. At the time, I felt as if I might prefer to have been soundly thrashed, in preference to one of Pa's lectures."

"Ah ... I see where your rectitude regarding the law and logic might have come from," Jack smiled. "So, that is your assignment for you both. I give into your possession a ring of keys, keys to the padlocks and front door of Bell House. Sort out what is behind this spectral haunting. I am certain, as are the joint heirs, Mr. Robert and Mr. Benjamin Bell, that there is some devilment afoot with regard to the Bell mansion." With a serious expression, behind which his good humor lurked, Jack added, "Safeguard the keys, and take every care, in getting to the bottom of the matter, James. Otherwise any sale of a tempting property in the nation is in peril of having some miscreants pull a fast game of deploying fake hauntings to drive down the price."

"As you command, Captain." Jim sketched out a hasty salute, and all of them laughed, companionably.

In the morning, he and Toby rode east, a well-beaten path to Richmond and Houston, a road which they knew well, through having traveled it for a number of missions. Jim also knew it very well himself for personal reasons. It was the road toward home, the tall house in Galveston, with the salt-burned trees and rosebushes in the front yard, where his father and mother lived.

Now it was also the home of his father's new junior partner in the practice of law; Jeremiah Nichols, a fellow prisoner in the hellhole of Perote, along with his father. Jeremiah Nichols was a fine fellow, who had found favor in the eyes of Rebecca Reade, who had been Daniel Reade's wife, and then his widow. That she had married a man of the steadfast nature of Jeremiah after nearly four years of widowhood spoke well of Rebecca, for marriageable women of pleasing looks and amiable nature were few and far between in Texas.

Many a widow could be forgiven for marrying again, as soon as the grave of their last husband was filled in. Very few women had the hardihood and determination to earn an independent living from their own property and enterprise. Jim liked and respected Rebecca for her steadfast devotion to his murdered brother Daniel yet found himself a little sorrowful over her remarriage. But Jeremiah Nichols was a good man, a dutiful and even-tempered soul who would make a good stepfather for Daniel's orphaned sons and small daughter.

It pleased Jim to see that Galveston – that pretty wood-built town which lined the inward shores of the long Island – had become a settled and thriving place. The shore facing the mainland was lined with a forest of masts, adorned with the flags of all nations, and the waterfront was lively and crowded in the late afternoon – sailors and stevedores laboring to load and unload cargo. Jim and Toby led their horses down the ramp from the little paddlewheel steamboat which had ferried them across the bay, bustling like a little doodle bug from landing to landing, collecting and dropping off passengers and their conveyances.

"It's too early for supper," Jim consulted his pocket watch. "I thought that we could go to my father's offices and see what he might know about the matter of the haunting. If anyone knows the latest gossip along the Strand, my father will know it. And what he doesn't know, Mr. Nichols likely will."

They led their horses along the Strand, and down Tremont Street where a small painted sign above the front windows of a tidy brick building advertised the services of Reade & Nichols, Att'y at Law.

"Jemmy!" exclaimed Jim's father, as a small bell on the door jingled, heralding their entry. "How splendid to see you, and Mr. Shaw as well! We did not expect to see you so soon after your last visit! Is a matter of national import which has brought you back to us … or simply a longing for the company of kin and the home hearth?"

"I wish that I could say the second," Jim replied warmly, as Jeremiah Nichols stood and smiled, a sheaf of documents in his hand.

"In any case, we're pleased as punch to see you both," he said. Jim grinned.

"Any excuse to return to Galveston – the richest port in Texas, and one of the few places in Texas where I am welcomed for myself, and not the office that I hold for Captain Hays! But we are here for a serious purpose, and we thought that we might pick your brains before we begin our inquiries regarding the so-called haunting of the Bell House."

Elisha Reade gestured the two Rangers to a pair of comfortable chairs, obviously meant for prospective clients, chairs into which Jim and Toby settled gratefully. Toby sat, silent and watchful, while Jim entered upon the first interview of their investigation.

"Oh, that," Jeremiah Nichols replied. "I am not entirely convinced that it is spirits, or some otherworldly and malicious phenomena. I am a rational man. Unless the spirit manifests itself in court and swears an oath on the Book, I will continue contending that it is the work of some malicious person. All the rest is merely tales, tales told to frighten children or the feeble-minded."

"Still, there have always been stories," Elisha Reade added thoughtfully. "About the Pirate Lafitte, and how he used voodoo magic to protect his treasure, and his Campeachy fortified establishment here. A regular pirate's nest, of outlawry, slave-trading, smuggling and worse. There was a moat around Lafitte's house. It was called the Maison Rouge, or the Red House. The Ball mansion was built over the side of that establishment. Lafitte lived like a king, and all the inhabitants of his colony swore fealty to him. Quite medieval, really. This occurred three or four years before your mother and I arrived in Texas, of course. By that time, the United States Navy enforced his departure, and his men burned the place to the ground before they departed. Like the tales of King Arthur or Frederick Barbarossa, he is supposed to live on, although most reports have it that he died and was buried at sea after being wounded in a battle with the Spanish off Honduras, some fifteen years ago. I suppose that it is possible he still lives under an assumed name, somewhere."

"The tales in the taverns and low drinking establishments have it that his men buried a large part of their treasure before they departed," Jeremiah Nichols noted. "The one that I have heard is that they filled up one of their cannons with gold coin, sealed up the mouth with wax and buried the cannon deep in the moat around the Red House."

"There were stories of Lafitte having left treasure all over Galveston Island," Jim pointed out. "Even when Dan and I were boys – I don't think there was an inch of land left untouched by a treasure-seeker with a spade."

"And little came of it," Elisha Reade added, with a professorial air. "To the best of my knowledge, none of them every found so much as a Spanish doubloon. But the stories of hauntings are new."

"Well, Dan and I found a couple of silver English six-penny bits," Jim added fairly. "But they might have been dropped by a sailor, rather than hidden by Lafitte."

"It is in my mind that tales of red-eyed hounds, and ghostly apparitions are a stratagem to reduce the price of the house," Jeremiah Nichols ventured, and Jim nodded, pleased that the man's active mind was coursing along the same trail as his and Captain Hays'.

"That is what Captain Hays suspects; someone wants to purchase the house and grounds for next to nothing and is chasing away buyers with tales of ghosts and haunts."

Elisha Reade shook his head. "It has always amazed me, that any thinking man might be frightened by such tales of the supernatural."

"True," Jim agreed. "But still – supposing that one has a wife, children or servants who are nervous about such tales. A man might think twice about having his household frightened out of their wits by stories told by the neighbors."

"True enough," Jeremiah Nichols acknowledged. "I myself would have liked to tender an offer for the Bell property, were it something that a simple man of law could afford in the first place, but I would not relish the prospect of Rebecca and the children living in such a place, thinking that every creaking hinge, or blowing curtain is evidence of restless spirits."

"So," Jim leaned his elbows on his father's desk and mused. "Tell us, if you know – who is most particularly interested in purchase of the Bell mansion. And if you have any thoughts about who is putting about the stories of spectral dogs and strange lights in an empty and shuttered house?"

"It's hard to tell," Jeremiah took a seat at his own desk. "Who knows how rumors spread! I suppose that servants gossiping and the slightly tipsy among their friends at the nearest tavern have much to do with it. Tracing such a rumor to an origin would be as fruitless as working out where the weeds in a garden have come from, once the seeds have been spread. As for interested purchasers, I think the most persistent is Henry McCallan, a gentleman from Scotland who wishes to purchase the mansion. He has shipping interests in Galveston, Barbados, and Jamacia. He is determined to drive a hard bargain for the place, being a tight-fisted Scot, but I cannot really see him as being unscrupulous."

"A hard man, but fair," Elisha Reade nodded in agreement. "Now there is also a Mrs. Fountain; Mariah Fountain, a widow from Bridgetown in Barbados. She speaks like an Englishwoman, but dresses in the French style, and appears to be of the highest degree of Creole Spanish. She has a son about seven years of age. Teddy. He is a schoolfellow of young Daniel's, which is how we know of the boy. She keeps a respectable boardinghouse in a quiet street. She would like to expand her enterprise into the Bell mansion, which is situated not much distant from her boarding house."

"There may be others interested," Jeremiah added, "But those are the ones who spring to mind at once."

"What of Madame Fountain's boarder, Mr. du Plessis? Now he is a curious one; he claims that was once an officer of

Napoleon's army ... but he walks with the rolling gait of an old sailor."

"Oh, he isn't one for buying the Bell place," Jeremiah Nichols leaned his elbows on his desk. "Although I have often noted that he often walks to a place where he can view the mansion. A man of sixty-something, with every year of a hard life engraved on a weathered countenance. He spends some minutes regarding the building, and then he sighs, shakes his head, and walks back to Madame Fountain's boardinghouse. Me, I think that he is a dreamer, building a castle in the clouds, imagining himself living the life of a king in that house."

"But he has not tendered a bid to purchase?" Jim asked.

"Not to my knowledge," Jeremiah replied. "So how do you wish to proceed. James?"

"With all care, and tomorrow, after a good supper, a good night's sleep and a change into clean clothes. I think to approach Mr. McCallan first. Can you tell me if he is in Galveston presently, and where his place of business might be, Pa?"

"Most often, he stays in rooms at the Tremont House," Elisha Reade began closing up his own desk. It was very obviously the end of his working day. "But he has an office in his company warehouse on the Strand at Bath Avenue. You cannot miss it, for it is painted entirely red, with a very fine sign of a painted sea-monster with a curling tail above the door. If he is not in his rooms, then enquire at that place. As for Madame Fountain, her boarding house is at the corner of the Strand and 15th – just a short walk from the Bell mansion.

A smallish house, painted white, with blue shutters and a gallery across the sides along the street. I believe that she is desirous of expanding her enterprise, as her current house is barely large enough to comfortably accommodate her guests."

"Then I will speak with her, as well," Jim decided. "Well, that's enough of business today, Pa. Can we hope that Fat Nella has cooked up her usual splendid evening supper for us?"

"Of course," Elisha Reade replied, for the free mulatto Nella, who was not really fat at all, was famed throughout Galveston for her cooking, especially her beaten biscuits. "And she cooks so generously that the two of you, even though being unexpected guests, will think yourself well-feasted, and never feel a lack at our table."

"Good," Jim and his blood-brother had traveled for all of a long day to reach Galveston, and begun their day before sunrise, on a meager breakfast of cold cornbread and slightly off-tasting fried salt-pork served at a crude boarding house on the shore of Trinity Bay. He felt himself to be near to starving; and his mouth watered at the thought of Fat Nella's superlative cooking. He and his father, with Toby and Jeremiah walked through the windswept streets, as the setting sun illuminated only the taller chimneys and steeples, while shadows filled the street below, save where a gap in the build-up part of the city let a few afternoon-gold rays of light to reach the dusty street.

The sun had almost entirely slipped below the horizon, during the short walk from Elisha Reade's office to the tall house with the open galleries and salt-burned garden, which had been the Reade house since the family had first arrived in Texas. The children; Daniel and Rebecca's two sons and their little sister were playing in the front yard, a round of children's games. All three ran, shrieking with excitement, once they spotted Elisha and the others, crying variously, "Poppy! Nuncle Jim! Papa Jeremiah! Mr. Toby!"

Jim could only admire, in some small astonishment, how much young Daniel seemed to have grown in the few months since he had last seen his nephew. So had Eli, the younger of the two, and Emily was the demure image of a seven-year-old Rebecca, grave and dark-haired.

"I don't come home often enough," he confessed to his father, in a quieter moment, as the children took Toby and Jeremiah's hands and tugged them toward the stairs.

"You're here often enough," Elisha replied. "As often as your duties permit – and that this duty takes you homewards – well, that is blessing enough."

"And that you can assist us in resolving it," Jim grinned as his father as they climbed the steps and went into the house, "Well, that is another blessing indeed."

At that moment, Jim's mother came into the hallway from the parlor, having heard the clamor of the children.

She embraced Jim, exclaiming, "Jemmy! What a marvelous surprise! I was going to write a letter to you, but I never know how soon or late you will receive it! What brought you to Galveston, so soon after your last quandary... and you have Mr. Shaw with you as well, so I suppose that is another matter of State business ... how long will you remain, then? Well, never mind. Come in, come in – are you hungry? Yes, I imagine that you are, darling Jemmy! I'm so happy to see you!"

"Yes, to all the questions, Mama dear," Jim replied, returning the fond embrace. "And I am happy to see you, and Rebecca and Pa and all the dear children! I don't know how long that Mr. Shaw and I will remain ... until we solve the mystery of the Bell mansion, I suppose!"

"Susan, my dear," Elisha cleared his throat. "The lads are hungry, and might we talk about their mission – as Jeremiah and I are hungry as well."

"Of course," Mrs. Reade replied, "And over supper, we can tell you all the news of Galveston..."

"That is what we hope for, Mama," Jim was at home in his heart, the refuge where womanhood ruled, the one place, aside from Jack Hays' house in old San Antonio, where he could always be assured of a welcome.

It was good to come home, setting aside consideration of their mission for several hours, to relish good home cooking, and the company of his family. When at last, Jim pled exhaustion from the long journey, he and Toby were shown to the largest of the guest bedroom, a room which opened onto the gallery through long French windows. Toby, as was his habit, took several blankets and stood on the gallery railing, looking down and considering the garden below.

"Picking out a good tree to sleep under?" Jim sat on the bed to pull off his boots. Toby shrugged.

"It would insult your mother's hospitality, for me to sleep in the garden, as if her roof is not good enough for me. I will settle on this; at least it is in the open air." He turned to face Jim through the tall glass doors, doors which stood open to invite the fresh ocean breeze to wander inside. What of tomorrow, James?"

"We talk to the Scot, Mr. McCallan," Jim replied. "If we cannot find him at his place of business, then we shall wait upon him at the Tremont House. And in the event that we cannot speak to him, then to Madame Fountain. We ask about their interest in Bell House ... but first, I think that we should go to Bell House, and search the premises, very carefully, for any signs of human trespassers. There are certain steps that we can take ..." he outlined what he intended to do, after their search of the Bell House – and Toby agreed, with a cheerful expression, before they lay down in their various blankets and sleep covered them over like a bank of sea fog, rolling in from the ocean.

Jim slept deep and longer than he had expected to – it was light, full morning daylight when he finally roused himself from that was the most comfortable bed that he had slept in for months. Both he and Toby were more accustomed to a rough camp, a bedroll under the stars, or what passed for a pallet on a crude wooden floor in some frontier cabin. To sleep between clean, starched sheets, smelling faintly of verbena – that was the highest luxury imaginable. When he went down to breakfast, it was to find his father already departed to the office, Toby in the summer kitchen, talking to Fat Nella's husband who was called Big John, although he was a wiry man of somewhat less than average height and almost entirely pure African – like Nella, a free Negro. But Big John was immensely strong, and earned a living on the docks, and doing whatever heavy work was required in the Reade household. Jim liked and respected Nella and Big John, but he could never feel as comfortably at home in their company as Toby could – the son of the house and of their employer – and the fault was not entirely his.

There would always be a sense of restraint in Nella and Big John's relations and conversation with him; a constraint, which was not there, with Toby. But he and Toby had slashed the palms of their hands, mingled their blood over a ceremonial fire and become brothers under the auspices of Mopechucope, the wise Old Owl of the Penateka Comanche, and that was all the difference. Jim had lost one brother and gained another. James Reade of Texas and Toby Shaw of the Delaware people stood shoulder to shoulder against all enemies, foreign and domestic, as he and Daniel might have – if Daniel hadn't been slain by treachery, all those years ago.

Only his mother and Rebecca still lingered over the breakfast table. Rebecca looked frazzled – as well the mother of three still-small children might. She was nibbling at her breakfast toast and a few small slivers of bacon as Jim's mother fussed over the coffee pot.

"I can ask Nella to fry you up more eggs," Mrs. Reade offered, and Jim demurred. "No, I'm fine with this. More coffee, though..." and Mrs. Reade took the coffee pot in her hand and vanished in the direction of the summer kitchen. In her absence, Jim looked at Rebecca and observed,

"Are you well enough, Sister Rebecca? You have shadows under your eyes. Sorry to say so, but I have been trained by the example of experts to notice such things."

"No, James," and Rebecca favored him with a rather uncertain smile. "I slept well enough – save for when Jeremiah had another nightmare. A nightmare where he relived some of his awful experience in the Salado battle, and then his imprisonment in that dreadful Perote place. Afterwards, I could not go back to sleep."

"He's a good man," Jim replied. "It troubles me to hear of this… there are memories which also give me uneasy sleep."

"I expect that most men who have experienced horrifying events have reoccurring and unwelcome memories," Rebecca observed. "What most calms Jeremiah is to go for a long walk, even in the middle of the night. He finds the darkness soothing, he says – to walk by the shore and listen to the waves and walk until he is tired sufficiently to sleep again."

"A good plan, I think," Jim replied. "For myself, I light a candle and read a chapter or two of *Blackstone's Commentaries* … it composes my mind."

At that moment, Mrs. Reade returned, bearing a freshened pot of coffee. She poured out a cup of it for Jim and another for herself, and settled back into her chair with an expectant expression on her face as she asked,

"Jemmy, what are you and Mr. Shaw planning for today? And do you plan for partaking of supper with us tonight? I will ask Nella to set places for you, if such are your plans."

"We should be home by then," Jim explained. "We plan to speak with both the prospective purchasers of the Bell House ... after a careful inspection of the house. We were given a set of keys to the various locks. If there has been a very corporeal presence trespassing there, we may find traces of their presence. And if not ... then we shall set some small traps. Might we trouble Nella for the ashes of last night's fire in the parlor stove? They should be cooled sufficiently by now..."

After a hearty breakfast had been consumed and appreciated, Jim and Toby together ventured to the Bell mansion, standing bleak and deserted in it's overgrown or never-planted garden. The morning fog dripped condensation from the leafless branches of spindly and discouraged small trees. Toby carried a small sack which once had contained flour, and now several scoops of finely sifted gray ash, gleaned from last night's fires. Fat Nella had been first indignant and then amused, when she was asked for the use of her best mesh sieve. Jim had the ring of keys in his coat pocket, his hand upon them, since he remembered Jack's admonition to keep them safe. As far as was known, they were the only existing set of keys to old Malachi Bell's grand house – and if such were not the case, Jim had every intention of discovering who did possess a set, or even just a single key. The stout wooden shutters over every ground floor window were nailed shut, a streak of red rust from the nails testifying that those shutters had not been opened for many a season.

"Seems sound enough," he remarked to Toby, as they crossed the veranda of Bell House, and approached the imposing front door. A circle of stout chain linked the two wrought-iron door handles, each in the shape of a leaping dolphin, the chain looped through the "D" of the creatures and secured with a heavy lock. The largest of the keys fitted into it, and turned, releasing the ends of the chain. Jim set his hand to one of the doors, and it swung open with a protesting creak. From the testimony of unused and salt-rusted hinges – no one had come into the Bell mansion by the front door for many months, if not years.

"If anyone has been trespassing, they didn't come in by this door," Jim commented, somewhat unnecessarily to his companion. "Well then, let's see what we can find."

At the end of two or three hours – nothing much save questions and suppositions. They walked on silent feet through all three floors of the mansion, a place shrouded in silence, dust, and the echoes of their quiet remarks to each other as the two young men passed from room to empty room. No curtains, no adornments hung on the paneled or plastered walls, little in the way of furniture. They tested the shutters on the downstairs windows – all latched fast from the inside, some of the latches much corroded and sealed together by the salt-dampness that crept in from the harbor, not more than half a block distant. The back staircase, intended for the use of servants, showed no signs of anyone having climbed up and down their narrow and steep steps. The grand main staircase, a continuous spiral connecting all three floors, was illuminated by watery light sifting in from a domed glass skylight in the roof.

"What a curious thing, James," remarked Toby as he looked up. "A window in the ceiling! Who could have thought of such a thing?"

"French invention," Jim replied. "After the ancient Romans, I believe. It will let in natural light yet keep the rain out. The late Mr. Bell imported the glass necessary for it at great expense. I can only suppose that this and other refinements are why the property is such a matter of interest."

The curving staircase did show a number of peculiar scuff marks in the dust, but not sufficient to give any definitive footprints. One curious finding was four 3-pound iron cannon shot, each roughly the size of billiard ball, wedged under the staircase, on the ground floor, as if forgotten by some absent-minded artillery company. There was no dust upon the cannonballs, which seemed unusual to Jim, as he studied one, weighing it in the palm of his hand.

"The nearest neighbors report odd sounds coming from inside," he ventured, finally. "I suppose that rolling these down the staircase from the third floor might make a curious kind of sound, as they fell."

Toby only shrugged. He disliked closed rooms and the insides of houses; only his interest in the mystery of Bell House kept him inside of this one. They sprinkled a thin dusting of ash in various places in the house, wherever they thought that a human visitor might tread, in the act of shining lights and rolling cannon balls throughout the property.

It was when they went to let themselves out again, and as they opened the front door, a stray beam of light, sliding into the hall from the doorway, fell on something – a crumb of broken glass which shone like a diamond.

"How very curious," Jim remarked. The fragment of glass lay on the floor of the hallway, below a single pane in what had been a sidelight: columns of glass panes on either side of the front door. A set of smaller shutters covered each of the twin sidelights, but now that Jim looked at them closely, it seemed that the lowest pane on one side had been broken. All those broken shards of glass had been cleared from the window setting and the floor beneath it, save for that small betraying crumb.

"Indeed," replied his blood-brother, who now was stooping to examine the narrow wooden shutter which closed off the glass sidelights. "James, come and look at this ... there is a way into this house. The lowest boards of this shutter are only barely held in. Look at this. See – the nails barely hold. I can slide them out with my bare hands." He suited action to words, pulling half a dozen loose nails from the shutter, revealing an opening about eighteen inches square.

"I do not think that anyone but a small child, or maybe a circus acrobat could get into the house, through this opening," Jim regarded the opening thoughtfully. Toby looked over his shoulder.

"An accomplished thief, perhaps – but one not broad through the shoulders."

"Well, put the boards and nails back," Jim said, with a resigned sigh. "So at least, our mysterious intruder will not see that his or her way into the Bell House has been noticed. Now that we have set a kind of trap for an intruder, let us now go and speak with the Scot, Mr. McCallan."

They departed from Bell House, after replacing the loosened panels and nails of that one shutter by the front door and strolled down to the Strand and Bath Avenue, searching for the warehouse with the red-painted sign of an ornate sea-monster over the main gate.

They soon found the warehouse that they sought, in that part of the Strand which faced the open harbor. A forest of masts loomed over the street opposite, a street crowded with stevedores and sailors horsing stacks of cargo from hold to shore. Gulls circled overhead, mewling their plaintive calls. The clean salt-smelling breeze mingled with the pungent scent of tar, human sweat, rotting wood and filthy bilgewater pumped from the holds of so many ships at anchor or tied up to the wharves and docks. McCallan's enterprise in Galveston was, as Elisha Reade said, marked on the Strand with a large sign swinging from a metal bracket and a pair of chains. The sign featured a painting of a gold and green sea-monster frolicking in a blood-red sea, a monster which might have been a whale at the fore end, but a dragon with a curly tail at the aft end. The only thing out of place was that the side of the warehouse compound back along Bath Avenue looked to have been marred in a patch by smoke and something fired below.

"Curious," Jim remarked, and his blood-brother nodded.

"As if someone tried ... without any success ... to burn the place," Toby remarked, after a searching look. "Or as if they merely made a threatening gesture. It does not seem that the fire made any progress at all."

"Interesting," Jim replied, and the pair of them walked approached the open gates to McCallan's warehouse compound.

The wide gates to the warehouse compound stood open; Jim and Toby entered without any hinderance. Indeed, hardly anyone appeared to take notice of them at all. The compound within seemed to be a busy, purposeful place. Of the first person they encountered – a workman with a barrow laden high with sacks of – something, perhaps refined sugar – Jim asked respectfully of the whereabouts of Mr. McCallan.

"Over there, I reckon," replied the laborer, pointing with a thumb toward the innards of the largest warehouse, the main door of which stood wide open. "Iff'n he ain't there, then in the office. Jist go up that there staircase. That door there, that's his office."

"Thank you," Jim replied with a nod. "We'll try the warehouse first." He blinked in the sudden dimness inside as soon as they crossed the threshold. The warehouse was piled high with crates and boxes, barrels, and neatly piled sacks, redolent with the scent of molasses, rum and sugar, the lingering hint of spices, dust and new-sawn wood overwhelming the salt-sea breeze. Four men in shirtsleeves labored, with many a shouted oath, at unloading a sledge pulled by a brace of oxen, supervised by a fifth; a man clad in a fine cloth coat and fine neckerchief. "I think that would be the one that we seek," Jim added, more certain of himself as he noted the fine beaver hat, and the resplendent red chin-whiskers. Clearly this man was no laborer and too finely dressed to be a clerk. "Sir – Mr. McCallan, I presume. Captain James Reade, Texas Rangers, my associate, Mr. Toby Shaw. Might we have a word or two with you?"

"Aye," replied the gentleman, abruptly. "But come to the point briskly, Captain Reade. I'm a busy man, with no time to waste on trivialities."

"Much obliged, sir," Jim replied. "Straight to the point – your interest in purchasing the Bell House?"

The gentlemen suddenly lost interest in the list of commodities in his hand. He looked at them very straightly and replied. "We will discuss this in my office, in privacy, Captain Reade. If you will follow me..."

He stumped away before Jim could reply; he and Toby followed the Scot across the compound and up the narrow stairs to a small office perched on the upper floor of a building which looked, from the wagons parked below and the corral full of horses and oxen meditatively chewing over their fodder, as if it were the stables for McCallan's enterprise.

The office was a Spartanly furnished place, with a single desk and half a dozen hard wooden chairs, none of them too comfortable, as Jim discovered once that he had taken a seat on one. Mr. McCallan, the shipping magnate took a seat on another – of equal discomfort and fixed Jim and his blood-brother with a hard glare. He had taken off the tall fashionable beaver, and his head was revealed to be entirely bald, save for a narrow fringe of red hair clinging to a circuit around the back of his head just above his ears. Jim could hardly tear his eyes from the spectacle. He had never yet seen a man so magnificently whiskered below the chin and so naked above it.

"It is no difficult matter, I would have thought, to have made a bid for a property," Mr. McCallan began, without preamble. "The Bell House would suit me well. I have residences in Bridgetown, and in Kingstown, for when I do business in Barbados and Jamacia. I have offered for the property, but there are certain... obstacles in the way of my offering for the Bell House. Certain threats against my warehouse and interests if I persist in my offer; an offer which I hold to my last breath, is a fair and honest one. How can a man do business, in a place where threats out of the shadows afflict the doing of honest business? There are shadowy interests at work here, gentlemen, which I like not!"

"What manner of threats and obstacles?" Jim asked, in a neutral tone of voice, and Mr. McCallan reddened with a fury which he had managed to suppress heretofore.

"My warehouse!" McAllen slammed his fist down on the top of the desk, and the solid piece of furniture shivered slightly at the impact. "My own enterprise in Galveston! Some miscreant sent me a message threatening destruction of the warehouse and my ships if I persisted in my offer to purchase the Bell manor! God, Reade! I regret that I ever heard of the place being on offer!"

"What, if anything, did they – these miscreants do – by way of demonstrating their power to deliver a threat, Mr. McCallan?" Jim asked, as calmly as was his practice – or the practice of his father, in cross-examination.

"They set fire to a barrel of pitch, rolled against the side along Bath Avenue!" Mr. McCallan's fury was no mild thing, but it glowed like the fire in a blacksmith's forge, fierce and of a degree to soften iron held in it's heart. Jim nodded; yes, he and Toby had observed the smear of char along that side of the warehouse compound. Obviously, it had been so recent that McCallan had not had time to order his workers to paint over the scar. "This, after relaying a threat in writing!"

"And how was that threat relayed to you?" Jim kept his voice level, calm, hoping that it might reassure the man somewhat, or at least tone down the degree of fury.

"It was not the first!" Mr. Macallan rage was not the least diminished. "Only the first which had any teeth in it, sirrah! The note in which it was contained was brought to me by one of the workers. He said it was given to him by a woman veiled in black, whom he did not recognize. But then, he wouldn't, since he is new-come to Galveston!" And Mr. McCallan appeared to chew on his generous mustaches, until Toby cleared his throat and inquired gently.

"But the previous threats you say that you received. How did they arrive?"

"I took no notice of them at first," The Scot replied. His temper was still at a gentle simmer. "I am a man of business, and as such – well, there are many who consider that I have trodden heavily on their toes, and bluster their resentment, usually over their cups. But I have never been crooked in my business dealings! I have been a fair and honest man, in all of my dealings, and no one, no one has ever thought fit to threaten me with fire and violence!"

"Ah. Perhaps you have not yet done sufficient business in Texas," Jim murmured. "For there are those among us who would play a slick game of cards with the unwary ... but yes, honest men have no need of or use for threats of violence or arson in the night. But my question remains;how did the previous threats to your warehouse in Galveston arrive?"

"Through written notes, sealed without any address or signature, delivered with the daily post or slipped under the door of the warehouse," McCallan paused and consulted his memory. "Some of them were handed to my workmen – the veiled woman, of course, or a small boy who ran away, without the man to whom he gave it taking any note of his appearance." McCallan shrugged wearily. "Boys of any age are everywhere, about the Strand and the warehouses. The ships and sailors draw them, like ants to spilled honey – the excitement of it all, gentlemen."

"Have you, perchance, saved any of those notes? Might we examine them for clues?" Jim truly didn't know what might be revealed, if anything, but surely something might occur to him. If anything, as one accustomed to considering evidence in a trial should be well-acquainted with paper and pen.

Mr. McCallan waved, dismissingly. "Be that as it may, Captain Reade. If you can deduce anything meaningful from those messages that I have saved, then you may be a wiser man than I am. If you can bring this vicious miscreant to justice, then so much the better. I am not a man accustomed to tolerating threats against myself, my enterprises, or my property." He turned toward the desk, and upon opening one of the cubbyhole drawers, took out a small bundle tied with a turn of blue tape.

Jim accepted the bundle and extended his hand. "Thank you for receiving us, Mr. McCallan. I cannot make any definite promises, but I do assure you that we will make every attempt in resolving this mystery."

"And the best of luck to you, Captain," Mr. McCallan grunted, not sounding as if he held out any great hopes. "If you wouldn't mind showing yourself out. Time is money for me, and I have little enough of the one to waste it."

Which was gracious enough for Jim, considering that he wanted also to speak with the other party most interested in the Bell House. He consulted his pocket watch. No, it was almost noon. If Mrs. Mariah Fountain ran a boarding house, likely she was caught up with overseeing the midday meal for her boarders. The afternoon would be a better time. In the meantime, Jim considered showing McCallan's collection of threatening notes to his father. The senior Reade had done business in Galveston for more than twenty years. Perhaps he might recognize the handwriting, or a turn of phrase. Therefore, they turned their footsteps toward Tremont Street, on the assumption that Elisha Reade and Jeremiah Nichols would be too busy with clients for a leisurely meal in the middle of the day.

When Jim unfolded the first letter and laid it on his father's desk, the senior Reade looked over the top of his glasses, and mused, "Most curious, my boy ... most curious indeed. Let me examine the others..."

Jim unfolded all the threatening letters; there were seven in total, all written in ink on good rag paper, which he found curious.

"I suppose I might go to the various shops in Galveston and see who sold this kind of paper..." he mused.

His father shook his head. "Almost everyone of quality would use paper of this degree. You'd be suspecting half the population of the city. Meanwhile, Jeremiah Nichols looked over his shoulder, still munching on the bread and cheese which had been his brief meal at his desk.

"I see what you mean ... look, some words look as if they were deliberately spelled wrongly, but later in the same letter, that same word is spelled correctly."

"But the fist is abominable," the senior Reade concluded after his scrutiny of the letters. "Which I find to be a curious anomaly... that someone with a store of excellent paper and a facility for writing veiled threats in a manner so as not to be actionable in court as threats ... should have such very bad handwriting."

"Oh, I think I can explain that, sir," Jeremiah swallowed the last mouthful of bread and cheese. "I believe whoever wrote these letters was trying to disguise their handwriting. Make it look as if they were barely literate by writing with their left hand, Assuming as I am, that their natural habit is to write as most do, with their right hand. I had a schoolfellow in Bastrop who broke his right arm, climbing a tree to steal peaches, and thereafter for the rest of his year in school had to hold a pen and write with his left hand ... that scrawl on those notes reminds me of that."

"Can you tell if the writer was a man or a woman?" Jim asked, "The other prospective purchaser for the Bell House is a woman."

Jeremiah shook his head. "No insight on that account. Sorry, James. What about Mr. McCallan? Could be twisty enough to write threatening letters to himself, in the hopes of beating the price down, or exciting sympathy?"

"I don't think so," Jim replied, slowly. "I don't see it – he is a busy man, and I don't think his anger or impatience with the matter of the Bell House could be feigned. He isn't that good an actor. All that he considers is on the surface in the instant. I don't read him as a man of artifice or subterfuge."

"Nor do I," Toby agreed. "A man of little patience. Should he take it in his mind that you are his enemy, he will stab you from the front. Not in the back, by treachery."

No further insights were forthcoming, and the hands of that plain clock on the wall of his father's office were already moving toward the hour of two in the afternoon. Jim gathered up the letters, refolding them carefully with the ribbon tied around the bundle.

"Well, then – now we go interview Mrs. Fountain," he said with forced cheer. "And hope that we eventually will find enlightenment. The Bell House is a fine property, and I would hope one that would have a better fate than notoriety as a haunted house!"

"As a rational man," his father replied, "I am not inclined to believe in ghosts, spirit apparitions, or spectral beings. Like Jeremiah, I hold that unless it can appear before the judge and swear to truthfulness before witnesses, I believe such beings are figments of a deranged imagination ..."

"Or such spirits are the result of indulging in too much of the spirits of a different sort," and Jeremiah chuckled. "I wish you luck in resolving this mystery, James." And his countenance turned serious. "I recall how you were able to solve the matter of my dear Almira's disappearance, and I have always been grateful to you for that."

"It was a ..." Jim didn't know quite what to say, for the resolution of that mystery had proven tragic, all the way around. "I am only glad that the matter of Almira ..." he floundered again, and Jeremiah smiled, a sad smile.

"I know, James. I know. And I am eternally grateful. A sad ending, to be certain, but despair is a goad which cannot be ignored, just as Almira could not ignore it at the end."

"If you are off to interview Mrs. Fountain," Elisha Reade sent a piercing look in the direction of his son, and toward his junior partner in law. "Then we can return to the interesting question of the Murtagh will, and the practicality of Mr. Murtagh's wishes..."

"We shall see you at supper tonight, Papa," Jim said, as he tucked the bundle of threatening notes into his coat and headed toward the door. He briefly regretted the comfort and security of the career which he had given up, upon accepting Jack Hays' charge to be one of his stiletto-men, for the greater good and all of Texas.

Would that have palled for him, he wondered, as he and Toby strode along the Strand toward the Fountain establishment? He supposed that it would have, eventually –

as domesticity wove tendrils around him and pulled him in. Better to work it out of his system, he supposed. No, he didn't really envy Jeremiah all that much.

"I have an insatiable curiosity concerning mysteries," he remarked aloud, and it was only a comfort that Toby looked sideways at him and replied.

"So you do, James – as have I. The Old Owl, and my uncles would have said that it was a duty the great spirit has laid upon us."

"As if I believe in a great spirit," Jim replied, for he was a skeptical man, much as his father was.

"My uncle would say, 'If you do not believe in a Great Spirit," Toby replied, "Then you should hope at least that the Great Spirit believes in you."

"A splendid metaphysical conundrum, then," Jim replied, and the two of them laughed companionably.

At the Fountain establishment, they were received in the front hall by a young girl in a calico dress, a dress covered by a voluminous white starched apron, who bobbed a curtsy, and showed them into what she said was the small parlor. There was, apparently another, larger parlor, where Mrs. Fountain's guests were accustomed to gather; the sound of hearty male voices and pipe smoke floated from behind the half-closed double doors to that chamber.

"The madam shall receive you here," the girl assured them in a frightened whisper, before she fled, after casting an apprehensive look at Toby, who although dressed faultlessly, civilized-fashion in dark coat, shirt and neckcloth above the waist, was never the less unmistakably a Delaware otherwise, clad below it in deer hide leggings, moccasins and breechcloth – that and the long braids of dark hair hanging over his shoulders, bound with leather thongs and a ruff of feathers.

"She must take you for a rampaging Comanche," Jim whispered, with a grin, to his blood-brother. "On the warpath, intent on loot and kidnapping fair young maidens to add to his harem."

"Ridiculous," Toby added, somewhat smugly. "I have no need of kidnapping, James. If anything, if I kept a harem of women – and my mother and uncle would have something to say about that! – the girls would be clamoring to join it."

"The ladies' delight of four nations," Jim replied. He and Jack had long been accustomed to comment teasingly on Toby's ability for attracting affections from young women – and sometimes not so young, at that. The ladies at their chili kettles in San Antonio's main plaza appeared to adore him unreservedly. "You will let us know, surely, when you have settled on a wife from among them?"

"Of course," Toby replied, and would have said more, but for the parlor door opening. They both rose, in respect to the lady who appeared in the doorway; a slender woman of some years who was not conventionally beautiful in her features – but who somehow managed to draw attention. She was primly clad in elegant widow-black, a plain white lace house cap pinned on her dark hair, and her eyes, as warm and dark as plum preserves, reflected wary intelligence. She would have to be a good and conscientious businesswoman, in the trade that she practiced as a respectable boarding-housekeeper.

"Mrs. Fountain..." Jim began to introduce himself and his blood-brother, but she interrupted him.

"Captain Reade, Mr. Shaw – yes, Annice told me you were paying a call and gave me your names. She said you told her the matter was of some importance. Do have a seat, but I must ask you to be brief and not waste time getting to the point of the matter. I have a large household to run, and little time to waste on trivialities."

"Certainly, Mrs. Fountain..." Jim momentarily lost the thread of his thoughts, in wondering why she unsettled him so, in a faintly pleasurable way. She wasn't anything in the least like what usually attracted him to a pretty girl. Perhaps it was her voice, low and musical, with a faint accent that he just couldn't identify. "We were sent by our commander, in the name of the Republic of Texas to investigate the supposed haunting of the Bell mansion. This 'haunting' is a matter of concern to the owner, who wishes quite earnestly to sell the property ... and because of so many stories of ghostly apparitions ... such offers received have been withdrawn. All but your offer and that of Mr. McCallan, the ship-owner. And now he is reporting that he has received threats to his warehouse and other interests unless he withdraws his offer to purchase the place. I ask you, in all earnest, Mrs. Fountain – have you also received threats against your boarding house and your boarders, unless you withdraw your offer for the Bell property? By what means – in messages such as Mr. McCallan received? And if so, did you save such communications?"

The Widow Fountain regarded them soulfully for a long minute. "I have received a few such written letters bearing such warnings, Captain Reade. They came to me by way of the post. I thought nothing of them once delivered, as I assumed they were for my boarding gentlemen. But I regret that I did not save them, once I realized what they threatened. I am a woman in business, Captain Reade. And as that, I am seen as a threat to many. From other women, jealous of my independence. And men, also jealous of such independence, and angry that there is no man who can force me to obey to heel and serve a domestic master. If that is all, gentlemen..." and she rose from the armchair in which she had briefly alighted. "I bid you good day. I am sorry I could not help you any further with his matter."

Thus dismissed, Jim and Toby had no other choice but to make a gentlemanly departure, shown out through the main door of the Fountain establishment by the same girl who had directed them into the parlor not ten minutes before. They stood on the front steps of the Fountain boarding house, adjusting their eyes to the bright afternoon sunlight after the relative dimness indoors. In the narrow garden between the Fountain place and the house next door, a young boy with a wooden sword fenced with a gray-bearded gentleman, similarly equipped; both laughing as they feinted, dodged and swung the wooden blades at each other. Jim smiled; it was a charming vignette of a boy the age of his older nephew, being indulged by a grandfather who was not as spry as he might have been once.

"I suppose that must be Mrs. Fountain's boy, Teddy – who is young Daniel's schoolfellow," Jim remarked, as they walked away. "And his old friend, du Plessis. What did you think of Mrs. Fountain? Was she telling the truth about the threats?"

"I cannot judge," Toby replied. "She seemed to be … evading any further questioning. She is not like any other woman that I have met. Not among my people, and not among yours, James. It is not an easy matter to read the tracks of a creature which one has never before encountered."

"We'll talk about it over supper," Jim concluded hopefully. "Perhaps something may occur to us then."

"In any case," Toby replied, with an air of satisfaction. "We still have left traps for an intruder at the Bell mansion. If we find evidence of a man and not a being of the spirits on our next visit, I will keep watch at night over the house."

"We both will," Jim assured him. "We will take it in turns."

"Curious, brother …" Toby looked back over his shoulder. "The old man … he holds the sword in his left hand. Do you think that significant?"

"Oh, probably just playing sword-dueling with the boy," Jim replied. "And didn't Jeremiah say something about how du Plessis had his right arm wounded, in his pirating days?"

There was nothing but pleasant conversation over supper, pleasant conversation and excellent food. No one could doubt that any dish which came from Fat Nella's kitchen could be anything less than fit for the table of the Queen of England. Still tired from the previous day's journey, and the conundrums presented by the day of investigating the Bell House, Jim and Toby were more than glad to take themselves upstairs and fall into their various beds.

Until they were woken in the wee hours by incoherent shouting in a man's voice from one of the other upstairs bedrooms. Jim hastily drew on his trousers, tucking the tails of his long shirt into the waistband, as he flung the door open.

The door to the room that Jeremiah and Rebecca shared stood half-open, golden candlelight flickering and casting shadows within. He heard the murmur of Rebecca's gentle protestations from within, as Jeremiah emerged, all but dressed and carrying his boots in one hand. Jeremiah's hair stood on end, every which way like an untidy haystack.

Over his shoulder, he was saying, "'Becca ... sweeting, I'm going to go for a walk ... oh, hullo, James. I guess ... sorry to wake you ..."

"You have bad dreams," Jim sighed. "Yes, Rebecca told me. I have 'em too, sometimes."

"I find that going for a walk helps," Jeremiah sat on the top step to draw on his boots. "I ... I do not want to distress Rebecca. I usually cannot readily return to sleep again, after one of those dreams."

"I'll come with you," Jim said firmly. "My own evil dreams often seem to be insubstantial things, under the stars. My brother ... that is, my Delaware blood-brother ... he claims that the open air in the wilderness brings healing. That alone under the sky, the Great Spirit speaks to you and brings a calmer spirit. Perhaps you can tell me what you dream of in the night, that unsettles your sleep. Rebecca worries about them, you know."

The two men let themselves out of the door to the house, together breathing in the night air, as Jim latched the door behind them. Inside the parlor, the repeater clock on the mantel struck the hour of two. The stars hung brilliantly in the sky arching over their heads. It was a clear night – a fresh breeze from the Gulf had swept away all the shreds of mist and fog which sometimes veiled the moon and the constellations. The moon itself was near to full, a chalk-white disc which sailed along the sparkling scarf of the Milky Way. As Jim and Jeremiah walked out to the street, an almost unseen shadow appeared, ghost-like, from among the garden. Jim was accustomed to the noiseless way that Toby walked on moccasined feet, and how his blood-brother could appear as silently as a shadow. Jeremiah looked over his shoulder, smiling as they went along the street.

"You too, Mr. Shaw? Are you also ridden by the nightmare, too?"

"At times," Toby replied. "There are things which in the daytime, I wish not to think of. But at night – those thoughts appear. Are we to walk long, James?"

"We are," Jim replied. After a long moment, he added, "Do not your friends among the Tonks call you 'The Long Walker?' I've always loved it here on the Island. The smell of the salt-sea... a desert, every much as the Llano, and the deserts between San Antonio and Laredo ... and points farther west. My mother's folk followed the sea, Jeremiah. And they came home from it with many grim stories to tell. When the womenfolk and the children weren't listening. When they thought that the children weren't listening ..." Jim continued conversing in that vein, as the three walked along the street – out to where the silver-edged waves lapped into the saltmarsh dunes that edged Galveston Island. He said nothing about the nightmare that rode him, when he was especially tired or ill; of waking in a daze, one leg pinned under his dead horse, and the bodies of his brother and the others of his Ranger company all dead in the dust nearby. It was Toby who had rescued him from death in the desert, burying Daniel and the others, tending him until he had recovered. Jeremiah likewise spoke little of his own helpless condition, surviving the massacre of the Bastrop militia after the fight with Woll's army at the Salado, only to be dragged away in chains to a brutal two years of captivity in a Mexican prison. Instead, they spoke of lighter things and casual matters; of the virtues of certain breeds of dog and horse, preferences in weaponry, and the correct way to bake johnny-cake over an open fire. They walked for several hours, until they were all weary, but in a good way, finally turning their steps back toward the Strand, and the distant forests of ship masts, bobbing at anchor in the bay, or tied up the wharves. Only a few lanterns showed golden in the dark night, most of them in the windows of a scattering of drinking establishments. The sound of discordant song came faintly to their ears. Otherwise, the city still slept, silvered by starlight in the darkest part of night.

"Sounds like some of the sailors are having a fine time of it," Jeremiah remarked, as they walked across the last sweep of sand toward town.

"Better them than me," Jim replied, heartlessly. He was tired; not only from several hours of a midnight tramp through the town and outskirts, but from the fruitless day that he and Toby had spent, attempting to unravel the haunting of the Bell mansion. At his side, Toby stopped mid-stride, raising his face like a hunting-hound at the first scent.

"James ... there is a light in the Bell mansion. A light where there should be none."

"My God, so it is!" Jim replied. They were at some distance from the Bell House, but it was clear in their sight. There was a dim, flickering yellow lamp glow from behind the shuttered windows. "There must be someone inside! If we leg it, we can catch them, red-handed!"

Their eyes had adjusted well to the darkness, so the three of them made good speed; even better when they reached the wide levels of the traveled streets. Toby, well accustomed to walking or trotting over long distances, was hardly short of breath when Jim and Jeremiah caught up to him – a barely seen shadow in front of the Bell mansion. Jeremiah, however, was puffing; obviously having spent much time behind a desk.

He gasped, "I don't see any lights now! Have they gotten away?"

"No," Toby replied in a whisper. "But listen ..."

Jim held his own breath, straining to hear over the pounding of his own heart. No, that was not his heartbeat. That was the sound of something heavy, like a series of iron cannonballs, rolling and bouncing down the curving staircase – a properly ghostly sound, like that of a distant cannonade, far out to sea.

"Part of the legend, I think," he murmured. "Whoever is haunting Bell House is still inside. And doubtless will emerge in a few moments once the work of haunting is done. All we need do is wait."

The three found places in the shadows cast by the trees and gateposts of Bell House, places where they could not be seen by anyone. They waited, while the silent stars wheeled overhead, and the clamor from those thirst-parlors on the back streets from the waterfront diminished to near-silence. After some twenty minutes, their patient vigil was rewarded. A small figure appeared to slither from the shuttered window that Jim and Toby had previously noted.

"Refastening the slats in the shutter," Jim whispered, and from his place in the shadow of the opposite gatepost, he knew that Toby had moved his head in a single nod of acknowledgment.

That small figure appeared; a shadow briefly outlined in faint starlight against the dark bulk of the building.

"It's a child," Jim whispered. "Just as we thought. Only a person small enough to fit through that opening in the shutter. The small figure darted down the front path, straight into the arms of Jeremiah, who exclaimed, as the child – for it was a child – cried out.

"Let me go! I wasn't doing anything!"

"Teddy Fountain!" Jeremiah said, almost in the same moment. "What mischief have you been up to! And no, I certainly won't let you lose! You've been up to mischief, and I want to know who put you up to it, for your antics have put these gentlemen up to a great deal of trouble!"

"I haven't done anything!" the boy insisted; he was very young, almost on the point of tears, but defiant.

"You were inside the house, the Bell House," Jim accused the boy most sternly. "We saw you, just now. Mr. Shaw and I were inside the house yesterday. We discovered the way that you have been using to go in and out. We shall find your footprints, everywhere that wee we scattered fine ash. This wasn't just boyish mischief, Teddy. This has serious consequences!"

"And even more serious when we tell your mother what you have been up to doing!" Jeremiah Nichols added, sternly. "Madame Fountain will not be pleased, not in the least. What if something happened to you? Your mother would be frantic, wondering if you had been run over by a cart horse, stolen away by the Comanche, or drowned in a ditch!"

"Grandpa Dupy would know!" Teddy insisted, mutinously. Jim could only think that the boy meant the elderly boarder, M. Du Plessis. He must be quite fond of the old man, and the old man of Teddy, to indulge him in mock sword play, as they had seen that afternoon on leaving the Fountain place.

"Unless ... did your mother put you up to this?" Jim was struck by a sudden insight. "Is she trying to beat down the cost to buy the Bell place, by spreading rumors that the house in haunted?"

"No! Not ..." Teddy blurted, and then it was as if he stopped himself from blurting out anything more. "It's not Mama."

"We'll see what she has to say to you then, young man," Jeremiah sounded quite the firm disciplinarian. "And we're going straight to your mother's house. She might not be awake yet, but I am certain that her cook, and maids have already lit the kitchen fires."

Teddy made no reply to that, walking between Jeremiah and Jim, with his head bent down. There was a faint, oyster-shell glow in the east, when they came to the Fountain place, not three blocks distant. To their surprise, there were lights behind the windows, the front door stood half-open, spilling more light onto the steps, where a single horse in the shafts of a covered shay stood.

"That looks like Dr. Smith has been called to attend someone," Jeremiah Nichols commented. "That's his horse and buggy, for certain. Hope it's not yellow fever; still too early in the year for it. That'll be bad for Mrs. Fountain's business."

"Bad for everyone's business," Jim answered, with a shudder. The dreaded plague spread mostly in the hot summer months along the coast and along the great Mississippi River, starting with the ague and a fever. Those fortunate few who survived their skin turning as yellow as lemon peel and puking black vomit never caught it again. This was not much comfort, considering the sufferings of those many who died of it in the heat of a humid summer, choking on smoke to banish the bad air.

Mrs. Fountain appeared in the half-open doorway, silhouetted against the light in the hallway behind her. "Teddy!" She exclaimed, "There you are – and where have you been? Mr. du Plessis has died! He fell ill and called for aid – and now he is dead! Teddy, darling, he called out for you at the last. He was worried about you, he wanted to say his last words to you, but you were nowhere to be found!"

And Teddy burst into tears, as did his mother, as she swept him into her arms on the threshold of the house.

"We found your son by the Bell House," Jeremiah began, as Mrs. Fountain half-turned in the open door.

"Thank you for finding my son," she said, over her shoulder, and firmly closed the door.

***

"Be assured, Jack," Jim said, three weeks later, upon returning with Toby to Bexar to report to his chief. "There is nothing haunting the Bell House, now. It was all down to a small boy, intent on a game – a jest to please an old man that he was fond of, and who indulged him by encouraging every sort of reckless adventure."

"And this old man?" Jack lit his pipe with a spill held briefly into the heart of the fire laid in the tiny corner fireplace of the old Mexican style house that served as his headquarters in Bexar. "This M. du Plessis? He died of a sudden fit of apoplexy before you could interrogate him?"

"Indeed," Jim sighed. "Curious, though; he was a Frenchy, with a lot of tales to tell, according to the boy. Tales of having been a soldier for Napoleon, or now and again a pirate king. He might have been a sailor, once, for some of the other boarders told us that he seemed uncommonly knowledgeable about the management of ships at sea. He was of a great age, and none of those stories quite matched up, according to what the boy told us, and what the other boarders in the Fountain establishment said."

"Might he have had any more motivation than sheer mischief?" Jack drew a deep breath through his pipe, setting the tobacco in it to briefly glow.

"I have a theory," Jim replied. "Only a theory, mind you – with little enough basis to go on. I wonder if du Plessis wasn't Jean Lafitte himself. He wanted his old house back again, or at least, the property. To live like the king of the pirates himself, in a grand mansion, if only he could sabotage the sale of it all!"

"Interesting," Jack drew on his pipe again. "But wasn't Lafitte supposed to have died in battle with the Spanish off the coast of Honduras and been buried at sea, twenty years ago?"

"It's what all the stories about him have it," Jim replied. "But what if they were just stories? He journeyed back to France, took another name, invented another past, and came back to Galveston, thinking wistfully about reclaiming his old citadel of Campechy? Madame Fountain ... aye, that's another theory to go on. Supposedly the deceased Mr. Fountain was one of Lafitte's junior cohorts, back in the day. But that's all a matter of conjecture, now."

"And why?" What's been happening concerning the Bell House?"

"That Mrs. Fountain and Mr. McCallan have decided to marry their fortunes and themselves together and purchase the property jointly." Jim replied, secretly amused that he had managed to surprise his commander for once and all.

"One has to appreciate a happy ending," Jack replied. "It's in all the novels. Now, I might have another mission for you and Mr. Shaw ..."

4 — The Fourth Adventure: The Death of a Disagreeable Man

"There's trouble brewing among the Delaware settlements at Fort Bird," Jack Hays remarked, one evening after reading several late-come issues of the latest newspapers from the east that afternoon. He and Jim were chest-deep in a cool quiet bend of the river, which lapped in sinuous reed-trimmed bends through Old Bexar. The day had been scorching hot, and a dip in the fresh cold waters of the river was the best means of cooling off and ensuring a quiet sleep overnight. "And Bob Neighbors has written to me about it. Edward Balfour has been doing his best to rile up white citizens against the Delaware and the Caddo folk. Dammit, they are our allies! They're just about to hold a grand peace conference, and that malicious fool Balfour is about to unload a stream of piss on the campfire. President Houston is furious, of course, and Bob is beside himself."

"General Sam would be," Jim replied, not a little indignant himself. Toby Shaw was not just his blood-brother, but his ally and fellow stiletto-man. Jim owed his life to Toby Shaw. If there were stouter allies and friends to Texans than the Tonkawa, Delaware, and Caddo scouts, then he would like to be introduced to them. "If anyone can bring peace to the frontier, it would be men like Bob. There's no one in Texas with more influence over the wild and the settled Tribes, or with more friends among them, than he has. Balfour is obsessive when it comes to Indians, wild or tame."

"Well, you might have some of that good influence yourself," Jack replied, with a swift grin. "So I am sending you and Mr. Shaw on a visit to Bird's Fort to visit his kinfolk, far out on the frontier. If you can stop at the Balfour place and talk some sense into the man, everyone, including President Houston will be grateful."

"What is Balfour getting riled up about now?" Jim asked, idly. Edward Balfour was something of an important man – a political ally of Mirabeau Lamar. He had several brothers, uncles, and cousins, most of whom held properties in the pine woods near Bastrop, and one *(a very respectable, charitable, and learned one)* who was a Methodist bishop. Edward Balfour was very much the black sheep of the family, as he had been elected to the Legislature several times as well as serving in the Bastrop militia company. Now he had a small ranch and a trading post far up in the unsettled lands – in fact, very close to where the various Delaware clans had established settlements on the Clear Fork near Fort Bird. Edward Balfour had narrowly missed being captured by Woll's troops after the fight at Salado Creek. He was famed for giving fiery orations when the Legislature was in session, and publishing even more sulfurous editorials in the *Texas Register*, or the *Austin Democrat* when it wasn't. He was famous for his detestation of all Indians, the Delaware, Tonkawa, Lipan Apache, and the Cherokee, who were friendly to the point of allying with Texas in fighting off Comanche raids, and generally living at peace with their white neighbors.

"He claims that he is being hunted and harassed for his views. Anonymous messages left at his house, scrawled in the dirt of his farmyard, his livestock mutilated. He claims that someone keeps shooting at his house, and throwing dead critters into his water wells. He blames the local Delaware folk, says they are all in on a campaign to persecuting him."

"Well, if I had made the whole Indian nation out to be my mortal enemies, and saying so in as many venues as Balfour has, then I shouldn't be surprised to hear that some of them take it as a personal insult and kick back," Jim remarked.

Jack nodded. "President Houston wants it all settled before the big peace pow-wow, even if you have to put a gag on Balfour. Figure out who is harassing him, stop them from doing so. If possible, make him sit down and remember his manners as a good Christian. Tell him in no uncertain terms to stop calumniating and harassing our Indian allies and friends with baseless and inflammatory accusations, or feel the very sharp pain of my displeasure, coupled with that of our President."

Jim sketched a wry salute; a very wry salunte, as he and Jack had stripped down to soak in the cool current, when the heat of a Texas spring afternoon had faded. Swimming in the river in the evenings after the sun had set was a popular summertime diversion in Old Bexar. A bath – and a means of cooling off. It was eccentric, but no more than the fad for sea-bathing among certain health fanatics among his father's neighbors in Galveston. Several young ladies, clad in cotton shifts which clung damply to their shoulders, waved, and blew kisses on their fingertips in his and Jacks' direction. The ladies were soaking in the pool at the back of the old Veramendi mansion, where several poplar and cedar trees dipped their knobby knees into the current, across the green river from where Jim and Jack were relaxing. A flock of birds made the evening raucous with their cries, as they settled into their roosts for the night.

"One more thing," Jack remarked. Jim sighed. There was always this 'one more thing' which Jack added, when it came to dispatching his stiletto-men on an errand of note. This was not a humorous 'one more thing' – he could tell from the expression on Jack's face. This was a deadly-serious 'one more thing.' "Balfour has been particularly eager to accuse the Shaw clan; our Mr. Shaw and his whole family, to include your blood-brother, as being the miscreants behind the campaign of harassment directed at him. Tell both Toby and Jim Shaw to take all care in your dealings in this. The Shaws, and all the Delawares indeed have a deadlier enemy than the wild Comanche, all too ready to rain fire and damnation down on him. Ed Balfour is as hot-tempered as he is hasty and indiscreet. And he has friends and a wide audience. Tread carefully."

"As I would, attending to a fire at the Powderhouse Hill," Jim replied, and he and Jack both laughed, before they swam upstream toward that place on the reedy bank of the river where they had left their outer garments, boots, hats and clean towels. "We'll ride for Bastrop and for Fort Bird in the morning, I take it. I shall tear Mr. Shaw apart from his ladylove of the moment and let him know what conundrum that we are riding into."

"Good," Jack replied. He waded out of the shallows, and looked to where the sun was setting, in the splendor of red and orange clouds edged with gold. "As always, I am confident that you and Mr. Shaw will resolve the situation to everyone's satisfaction. God knows, the two of you have resolved much tricker matters before this."

"Pleased that our commander has such trust in us," Jim replied, his mind already running ahead to the matter they would face at the end of the journey to Fort Bird. Yes, he would most certainly consult with Bob Neighbors; the expert in Texas in all things to do with the Tribes, both tame and wild. And Jim Shaw, who was the chief among the Texas Delawares, if truly anyone could be said to hold that office.

The next morning, Jim and Toby set off; the trail that led northwards, to where the settled fringes of Texas raveled out to the wild frontier, a frontier peopled only by wandering bands of Comanche. Who, if one was lucky, were only on the hunt for buffalo, or with their families and horse herds, moving to a new camp. When they rested their horses at noon, in the shade of an ancient pine tree at the edge of the upland woods, Jim relayed his worries about this mission.

"It's going to be tough," he finally concluded. "A test of diplomacy ... and puzzle-solving."

"Indeed," Toby agreed. "My uncle is a proud man, and we are born of a proud people. Not inclined to accept insult from a white man, specially not a man like Balfour ..." he frowned. "This is not that Balfour who has opened a school in Richmond to train ministers of the white faith?"

"No – that's his uncle. A worthy and gentle man, although fierce in the pulpit. This is the younger Balfour who was in the

Legislature, and sends fiery letters to the newspapers, condemning all Indians, tarring them with the same black brush, as not being fit to live in the same country with civilized people."

"Ah." Toby's expression was carefully inscrutable, yet Jim could interpret it very well.

"I think that if we go first to Balfour's holding on the San Saba, then you should pose as a white man; a frontiersman who has taken on Indian habits and dress, for the time of a short visit in daylight. We shall calculate to arrive in mid-morning. Then, you should ride on to your uncle's camp after a few hours assisting me, and I shall stay at Balfour's as long as it takes me to sort out who, if anyone, is tormenting the man. Failing that, I shall try and talk him down from whatever high branch of outrage that he has chosen to perch upon."

"Like an angry cat," Toby nodded, in perfect agreement. "Indeed, I am no more eager to spend a night under that Balfour's roof than he would be hosting me. Do you and Jack believe that someone is trying to kill him?"

"I'd not be surprised in the least," Jim replied. "Men that obnoxious often do have people who want to kill them. It's just that most civilized folk don't yield to the temptation."

As calculated, they came upon the Balfour place shortly after dawn, having camped the night before in a thicket of scrub oaks a short distance from the Balfour trading post. Jim had to admit, even if only to himself, that Balfour had picked out a nice piece of land for his establishment. The ramble of buildings was on a rise of ground shaded by several tall oaks and sheltered from the fierce blue northers, the main house and trading post oriented to the south. There was a fenced patch of corn, already grown to shoulder-height to a man, a similarly-fenced vegetable garden, and even a row of what looked like flowering shrubs – roses and the like, creamy white, yellow, and pink blossoms.

Jim thought as he and Toby rode down from the next hill, the morning shadows laying across meadows splashed with pools of colorful wildflowers – pinks, orange, yellow, blue and white, which made a wilderness garden which put the meager row of shrubs pitiful in comparison. But even so, the Balfour holding presented a picture of prosperity. Jim noted with a eye trained to defensive measures on the frontier, that the buildings – house, stable, wellhouse, a smokehouse with a threads of gray smoke leaking out of every crack and cranny, the trading post and blacksmith's open-fronted shed were all connected by palisade fences. The narrow windows in those buildings which had them were all covered with stout wooden shutters, shutters which now stood open to the cool morning air. He did not doubt that there were shooting holes in the upper walls of the house and the trading post.

There was a woman in a calico dress and a slatted sunbonnet, bending attentively over the rows of new green rows in the vegetable garden. She looked to be pulling up weeds which had sprouted inconsiderately among the planted rows. A young man – a boy, really, as Jim saw upon approaching the nearest building – was sweeping the floor of the porch with a long twig broom. He surmised that it was the trading post-general store. The large blockhouse behind it must be the main house. It had a sturdy, four-square and fortified look to it, which was sensible indeed, considering how vulnerable that settlements on the frontier were to attacks by Comanche raiding parties out for glory, horses, goods, and slaves.

"Good morning, friend," Jim sat at ease in the saddle a careful distance from the trading post. "Is this the Balfour place? I'm James Reade, of Colonel Hays' State Rangers, and my partner, Mr. Shaw. Is Mr. Balfour about? Mr. Edward Balfour?"

"He is," the boy replied, resting his chin on the end of the broom staff. "But he was feeling poorly this morning, didn't get up for breakfast. He took his tonic and went back to sleep."

The woman who had been weeding the garden had noted their approach, stepping carefully across the rows, each of which boasted a ridge of green; feathery or leafy, pale or bright, as was the wont of early vegetables. She came to the fence and addressed them in somewhat apprehensive tones.

"I'm Mrs. Balfour, Mr. Reade. If you would come to the house, I'll see if Mr. Reade has recovered enough to receive visitors." She was a pale, indecisive young woman, very thin. Her fingers moved like pale spiders on the handle of the weeding fork and the basket of pulled weeds that she held. She wore an enveloping apron of undyed homespun over a full-skirted calico dress with bell-shaped sleeves, almost in the latest fashion,

"Thank you, Mrs. Balfour," Jim doffed his flat-brimmed hat in courtesy and nodded toward Toby. "I have a matter of some import to discuss with him and appreciate the offer of your hospitality."

Mrs. Balfour vanished around the side of the trading post. Jim and Toby waited a decent moment before riding up to the main house and securing their horses.

Toby remarked in low tones, "She does not appear confidant in her position, as the wife of a propertied man. Why should this be so, my brother?"

"Likely because she was married to him as a trophy. The prize of womanhood suitable to what he thought of as his position in society."

Toby grunted; Jim knew his blood-brother well enough by now to correctly interpret that as an indication of his disapproval. Among the Delaware, women held and managed a family property and wealth, for the benefit of her children. Husbands might be warriors and leaders of other men, but women ruled the hearth and her children and controlled the real wealth. The young man with the broom had set it aside and came to take the reins of their horses.

"I'll put your horses in the corral, sir. Don't worry none. I reckon Ed – Mr. Balfour – will rouse himself to talk to Jack Hays' men,"

"Thank you, Mr. ..." Jim replied, and the young man grinned.

"Seth Kinderhook, sir. Sadie – Miz Balfour is my sister. Ed has me managing the trading post, day to day, since he is that busy, most days."

"Thank you, Seth," Jim replied. "Be careful of my pinto-pony; he has a jittery temper, and sometimes he bites at strangers who are too rough with him."

"That's all right, Ranger Reade. I'm good with horseflesh." Seth's eyes slid sideways toward Toby. "Your partner ... he ain't by chance an Injun, is he? Ed won't like that – he has a powerful dislike of Injuns. And I'm not real fond them, myself ... our oldest sister...."

"Mr. Shaw is of the Delaware, an ally to our folk," Jim replied, firmly, seeing that the boy was clearly embarrassed. "And I trust him with my own life; a life which he has preserved on occasions too many to count. Your brother-in-law can like it or lump it. Now, we are present here to investigate threats against the life of Mr. Balfour as well as to investigate certain accusations that he has made against those settled Indians. This is a matter of interest to President Houston and the nation. If you will take our horses to your corral and frankly answer Mr. Shaw's questions regarding these threats against your brother-in-law."

With a nod toward Toby, his partner went with the boy and horses toward the corral and stable yard. Jim and Toby had worked so long together in concert that very few words need be said between them. Jim waited a courteous moment on the porch of the blockhouse; a porch too skimpy and ill-furnished to truly be called a verandah, before knocking at the main door. In a moment, the pale young woman opened the door.

"I don't want to see anyone, Sadie! I am unwell, I told you!" a man inside the parlor spoke crossly.

"It's Mr. Reade from the State Rangers," Mrs. Balfour sounded apologetic. "He said they had sent him special, because of those Injuns at Fort Bird harassing you. I think you ought to talk to him, Mr. Balfour. P'haps he can sort it all out."

"All right, show him in," the cross voice replied from within, and Mrs. Balfour stepped back from the doorway, admitting Jim into a room which appeared to be fitted out as a study or library. Shutters half drawn over windows filled with oiled paper kept the place dim. After the bright morning outside, it took some minutes for his eyes to become accustomed well enough to see the face of the man enthroned in a cushioned chair with a robe over his knees. He had a gaunt appearance and scanty hair, which made him seem aged and frail, although from what Jack had related, Edward Balfour was only a little older than Jim himself. Mrs. Balfour took a chair in the dimmest part of the room. Jim almost forgot that she was there.

"Good of you to receive me, Mr. Balfour," Jim said, squinting into the dimness. "Sorry to find you so poorly."

"It's about time that someone in authority took notice of the threat posed to me by whose vile characters!" Ed Balfour's eyes narrowed to malevolent slits. "But you, Mr. Reade – you have a halo about you! I have made notes, extensive notes about those incidents. If you wish to review them ..."

"I had rather ask you directly," Jim replied carefully. "As you may explain or elaborate on your suspicions. You an important man in this part of Texas and not without influence. It has been my sad experience that such men often attract enemies, often through no fault of their own. Can you relate for me the history of those threats ... and what led you to believe that folk like the Delaware and the Tonkawa hold a particular animus against yourself?"

"Because they're damned, treacherous scourges of all civilized men!" Ed Balfour pounded his balled fist against the arm of his chair. "Oh, that fool Neighbors might believe every word of the fairy stories that his so-called tame Injuns pour into his ears, but I know better! Damn!"

To Jim's discomfiture, Ed Balfour sprang up from his invalid chair and rushed out of the room. Mrs. Balfour hurried after her husband, whispering what sounded like an apology. Jim waited, courteously, trying not to hear the sounds of vomiting from the farther room, but Mr. Balfour did not reappear. Jim was about to follow and offer his assistance, for the man sounded to be in very real distress; groans and other miserable sounds came from the farther room, accompanied by feminine murmurs of concern.

Finally, Jim called, "Mr. Balfour, are you unwell? Do you wish to continue with the interview?"

"I cannot, Mr. Reade! Not today. Speak to my wife or ask your questions of my brother-in-law regarding those threats and depredations!"

In a moment, Mrs. Balfour emerged from the inner room, wiping her hands on the apron.

"Has your husband often been ill like this?" Jim asked with deep concern, and Mrs. Balfour shook her head.

"Oh, frequently, sir. I have made a regular herbal tonic for him, which seems to help. He is resting quietly, now." She had a small bottle dark bottle in her hand. Going over to the tall desk in the corner of the parlor, she put the bottle down and took a bundle of papers wrapped in a length of ribbon from it, explaining, "Mr. Balfour has often been in ill-health; so much of the management of this house falls to myself and my brother. My brother and I are accustomed to carry on without him when he has these spells. Perhaps Seth can answer your questions. Mr. Balfour does not speak much of his concerns to me, saying that I am a woman and should not concern myself with such worldly matters. But he did say that you were to have these notes of his, to assist in investigation our persecution at the hands of his enemies."

"Thank you," Jim replied, thinking with some relief that he would not have to spend much time with the unpleasant and sickly Edward Balfour. He could review the notes, perhaps ask some questions of young Seth, and then get on with the second part of the task at hand; travel on to Fort Bird to sort out whatever grudge that Balfour had with Bob Neighbors and his tame pet Indians.

He found young Seth and Toby Shaw leaning their elbows against the fence of the corral, watching the horses chomping moodily on a manger of hay and shriveled carrots.

"Mr. Balfour was suddenly taken ill, as we were about to talk about those threats received." Jim announced. "But I have been given his packet of notes about those incidents. And he told me that you might be able to shed some light upon these threats and acts against his interests and property – which he has blamed the settled Indians for, at some length and with considerable venom."

"Yeah, he would that," young Seth looked down and stubbed his toe at a clod of dirt at his feet. "He's got a powerful grudge against the Comanche ... all them wild tribes, come to think on it. They killed my sister and our Pa, some ten year ago it was. Ed still carries that grudge like a big ol' stone on his back. That Sisyphus character in them old books? Ed don't got a patch on that."

"Your sister?" Jim queried gently. He was baffled, wanting to get to the bottom of this, and then to leave as soon as possible. "I thought that Edward Balfour was married to your sister."

Seth shook his head. "No, that was our oldest sister. Sabrina was her name. Tall and beautiful; the prettiest and sweetest girl in Bastrop and Ed was gone on her. The Balfours had the next place over. We all lived way outside of Bastrop then. Ed and Sabrina were to be wed. Date was set, Ma an' Sadie had the wedding quilt all but finished. Then one morning, before sunrise, Sabrina an' Pa went out to the barn to milk the cows and let the horses out to pasture. The Comanche hit our place, just then. Ma an' Sadie an' me, the hired men and our two slaves, we had just enough time when we heard the shots to close the shutters and fort up inside the house. They never got us," Seth gulped. "But they killed and scalped Pa. And Sabrina ... they did things to her. Wicked things. We could hear her screaming. She died hard, Mr. Reade, an' the worst of it was there wern't nothing we could do. It was a big war party, they had the house under siege. When they were done with her, they took her hair an' Pa's and rode away with all of our horses. Ed ... he never was the same, when he saw what they had done, what they left of her. He went a little crazy in the head over Sabrina. He was never that fond of Injuns before that, an' he turned plumb murderous afterwards. An' truth is, I've come to think that Ed blamed us in a way for how Sabrina died. After he married Sadie, he never missed a chance to say things, make her feel small. Me too, although I don't rightly know what he thinks that we ought to have done that morning. I was barely old enough to wear breeches. Sadie, she was only twelve when the Comanche killed Pa and Sabrina." The boy colored, in embarrassment. This had the air of a confession. "Sadie always had a shine for him, anyway, although he was Sabrina's beau. And we were grateful at first that he took care of our family place, what with Pa dead. Ed gave us all a home, a place to live, married Sadie … but it's been right awkward of late. If it weren't for Sadie, I'd have left here and gone to look for work elsewhere."

"Ah," Jim nodded; it made a kind of sense now. A warped sense – but sense. If it were possible, he disliked Ed Balfour even more, and he struggled against that. Law was law, right was right. Personal dislike had no right to sway justice one way or the other. "That adds considerable to my understanding of the situation. Now, your brother-in-law had a lot to say about persecution, threats … even claimed that Mr. Shaw's folk had opened a vendetta against him – petty harassment, thievery, poisoning his wells, thieving stock and all. What do you know of this? Mr. Balfour has made quite a name for himself in alleging all of this and more."

The boy was shaking his head, "Honestly, Mr. Reade, I don't know that there was anything of the sort. All those happenings which Ed blamed the Injuns for; I couldn't see anything in it. Sure, there were times when Ed got sick after drinking well-water ... but none of the rest of us did, an' we drank the same water. A couple of chickens dead? That was racoons – you'd know they are murder on chickens. We ain't misplaced no cows, either. Not in the last few years, save a few wild ones that wandered off on their own. Sadie's garden got torn up ... well, that was deer, to judge from all the tracks. Those damned rats with hooves got over the fence an' ate their fill." The lad shook his head again and regarded Jim with honest eyes. "We keep a pretty good watch on this place. Me, and the hired hands. Some red-skinned devils – sorry, Mr. Shaw – getting onto our place to cause mischief? I just don't see how it could happen. We keep a pretty tight guard, me an' the hands."

"So, what do you think is the cause of all this?" Jim asked, touched by the honesty in Seth Kinderhook's expression, and the lad shrugged.

"I can't honestly say, Mr. Reade. I honest-an-truth can't. I hate to think that Ed is wandering in his wits, but I'm certain-sure that he is, now that he's gotten to be so ill."

Jim exchanged a brief look with his blood-brother; yes, this made sense; that in his frequent illnesses, Ed Balfour had become plagued by fancies; fancies of persecution. Jim said, "I'm almost certain that is the case, and I will tell Captain Hays so, and hope that Mr. Balfour will cease pestering us all with these irrational fancies." He was struck by a thought.

"Perhaps you and Mrs. Balfour can intercept any letters and articles which he might write and send to the newspapers for publication, as such only serve to inflame the public generally."

"We'll see what we can do," Seth replied, although the lad sounded uncertain; as if he was reluctant to hamper his brother-in-law in any way.

"It is a matter of the highest concern," Jim pointed out, "That nothing shall interfere with the upcoming negotiations at Fort Bird, between the government of Texas and the various tribes. A treaty resulting in a permanent peace along the fronter is a matter much desired by all our peoples – and were Mr. Balfour of a mind to realize that … well, that would be most desirable outcome for us all."

"I dunno," Seth's expression was dubious, but at least he seemed willing to consider. "Hate has a good grip on Ed, but me an' Sadie, we'll do what we can."

"Good. And thank you," Jim clapped Seth on the shoulder. "Me and Mr. Shaw, we'll head on to Fort Bird, now that we've said our piece. Mrs. Balfour seems as though she has a lot on her plate today, so we'll not add to it by asking for hospitality." Besides, he was not very keen on staying at the Balfour place, not when they had the second part of their mission to attend.

Jim and Toby continued their journey north to the frontier, and the outpost of that crude fort established by Colonel Bird of the small regular Army of Texas some years previously; a fort intended to firmly peg down the boundaries of the nation. After several days of rough traveling across the wilds of northern Texas, they were both glad to reach the San Saba, where the larger part of the Delaware Indians in Texas had settled. Perhaps not as settled as the coastal lands, but not as wild as the Llano country, where the defiantly wild Comanche roamed at will, taking what they wanted.

They were welcomed by Toby's mother, who had taken the white name of Sarah; a handsome lady of middle years, as serene in her authority as an ancient Greek priestess, who ruled her branch of the Shaw clan and her household of younger women and children with an iron hand, swathed several layers deep in velvet glove, beaded in the old Abenaki style.

"My son, it has been long since you have visited us," she stood at the doorway of her household cabin, with a gaggle of small children clustered at her moccasin-shod feet – a majestic mother hen with her flock of small nestlings. "But you are welcome, as always, as is our son-adopted-of-blood. Welcome, James – you are indeed welcome ... you are not yet hand-fasted? For shame, for shame! You both should have wives, since you are young and vigorous; it is not fitting that young men should be without wives to adorn their lodges and bear children for the clan. Otherwise, you will fall into careless, dissolute ways and that is not good for The People. Or for my sons."

"Mother!" Toby protested, and to Jim's secret amusement, his blood-brother seemed to be flushing with embarrassment; Toby who was handsome, gallant and the love of the ladies of at least three nations. "I will do as you say – but not now. I will find a wife of my own; do not fear. And

James will do also. It is that now we are bound to serve for Captain Hays, sent hither and yon on such missions as he has detailed for us. We cannot marry at the moment, for he has said again and again, that there are things which he may only ask single men to perform, lest we leave a widow mourning, cutting her hair and slashing her breasts. It would not be fair,"

"Indeed, my son," Sarah Shaw seemed to agree, but with reluctance. "And are you visiting us as part of a mission for Captain Hays, this time?"

"We are so," Toby agreed, looking a little abashed at being read so easily. "We were asked to look into a matter of accusations made against our People by Mr. Edward Balfour."

"He has claimed that your folk were trespassing, poisoning his well by throwing filth into it, stealing cattle," Jim explained, seeing Mrs. Shaw's puzzlement. "Captain Hays wished to know the truth of the matter, and perhaps discourage Balfour from making false accusations, which inflame Balfour's friends. As if there was anything which might inflame feelings among our folk any more deeply than raiding by the wild Comanche! There is nothing but peace between ours and our friends among the Delaware, the Tonkawa, the Lipan, and the Cherokee; all inclined to walk the path of peace. The words of Edward Balfour might poison that peace – and thus, has the interest of President Houston."

"I know nothing of this matter," Sarah Shaw pursed her lips, as if to prevent her frank opinion of Edward Balfour escaping through them. "And knowing nothing, I will keep silent. Your uncle will know more of this matter, so you should speak with him at the feast tonight."

"A feast?" Toby's usually impassive countenance brightened with interest. "A celebration – for my return?"

"For your uncle and the birth of another child by his wife – a strong healthy boy," Sarah Shaw replied, austerely, and Jim could have chuckled for the way that Toby's face fell. Ah, well – never mind. It might prove amusing, seeing his blood-brother reminded yet again, that he was only one of his mother's sons, and James Shaw's many nephews.

"Spread your blankets in the room with your brothers, my sons," Sarah Shaw advised the two of them. "But before sundown we shall go to my brother's house. I would say to ask your questions of him, and perhaps see what Mr. Neighbors and Doctor Ford have to say?"

"John Ford is here?" Jim was astounded. John Ford was a person of consequence in Texas; not only a doctor, but qualified to practice law, and elected to the Legislature as well. He also owned a newspaper, the *Texas Democrat* – and as such, was a firm partisan of President Houston.

"They are guests of your uncle," Sarah Shaw replied austerely.

And so they were; Rob Neighbors, who was as gangly and enthusiastic as he had been when Jim first met him, in the adventure to the old San Saba fort some years previous. Rob – a survivor of imprisonment in Perote Prison along with the senior Lawyer Reade, had taken to the frontier and friendship with the Tribes as if he were a duck just discovering water and the kinship of his kind. There was not a man in the whole government of Texas who had more friends among the

Tribes, wild and settled, or more influence among them. Jim did not know what he should expect from John Ford, save that his father had described him as restless and the most intelligent man he had ever encountered. No small accolade from Elisha Reade, whose knowledge of the finer points of law was encyclopedic, and whose moral courage in the face of cruel injustice was a byword among those who had been imprisoned with him in Perote.

The celebratory feast was every bit as lavish as could be expected among the settled Tribes – some of the flavors and customs as alien and exotic, but Jim had become accustomed to them all, serving as Captain Hays' reliable stiletto-man. Hospitality was hospitality, no matter where it was staged, friends were friends no matter what their tribe or color, and food was good, no matter what the dish or the spices that flavored it. However, Jim and Toby both drew the line at the ritual of the Tonkawa after a successful battle – eating the flesh of the defeated enemy. Fortunately, the Leni-Lenape Delaware had no such custom.

Bob Neighbors was in his element; having been a prisoner in Perote for three long years, he had embraced the wild freedom of life among the tribes with increasing energy. During that evening, Jim watched wistfully as Bob and Toby were embraced by friends and kin, always in the center of a happy, rowdy circle under the circling stars and bonfires which sent golden sparks upwards to meet their silver cousins. James Shaw, chief of the Texas Delaware, was a solicitous host to all of his guests. As for himself, he and John Ford lingered more on the edge of that throng.

"I'll need to speak to you about Ed Balfour," Jim had said, at the beginning of the evening. "But tomorrow is fine – I don't want to spoil your party by talking of business matters."

"Tomorrow, then," James Shaw replied; he was a handsome, broad-shouldered man with a shrewd and worldly countenance. Only Sam Houston and Jack Hays stood higher in Jim's respect. His hospitality and regard were much warmer and more comfortable than that of the Balfours, and the assembled company much jollier and welcoming.

"Have you known Chief Shaw long?" Asked John Ford, with great interest, and Jim replied,

"A few years. My blood-brother is one of his many nephews. I did not meet him in person until several months after he and I became part of Jack Hays' stiletto-men."

"He's a good man," John Ford nodded in agreement. "One of the finest men in this part of the frontier – or so says Bob Neighbors. Bob thought that I should meet and get to know Shaw's people."

"So that is what brought you to the far frontier," Jim chuckled, and John Ford's lean and angular countenance took on a serious expression.

"I've been in the way of practicing the medical trade," he replied. "Since a study of the medical arts seemed to be within the grasp of any intelligent person. Bob wished me to come out to consult among his tame Indians about the practice of inoculating against the smallpox. My readings on the subject have indicated to me that they are terribly vulnerable to those diseases peculiar to our civilization."

"I don't think that the wild Indians have it any easier," Jim replied. "It's a harsh life, as I have come to learn, through our friendship with Old Owl and his people. They live for war, raiding and the hunt ... but they will starve at the end of a bad winter, if they have not hunted enough buffalo. Their lodges are simple skin tents. Their women bear few children who survive. Some say that is why they must take young captives and train them up in their ways, because they have so few children who survive to adulthood."

"It could very well be so," John Ford agreed. "And it would make a cruel kind of sense. I am hoping that Bob can convince his Indian friends – wild and tame alike – to consent to inoculation against the smallpox. Such a practice might alleviate some of the hardships of that life."

At about mid-morning the following day, Jim and Toby went to consult with James Shaw, regarding Balfour's accusations against them. Half a dozen older men of the settlement also attended, sitting on the ground under a huge oak tree with many gnarled limbs. Bob Neighbors was also in attendance.

"I knew of Balfour's attempts to rouse a rabble against our friends," Bob remarked. "I just couldn't see it, myself."

James Shaw snorted, in a scornful manner. "I cannot say that my people cared enough about Balfour to harass him ... and even so, we knew that any such acts that could be blamed on us would be taken up by him. No, Mr. Reade – I have heard nothing of our folk entertaining themselves by playing wicked pranks against him. Besides, his holding is three days ride from here – a long journey, when we have better things to do."

"It is not unknown for the Comanche to deliberately route their raids so as to cast blame on the settled Indians here," Bob Neighbors pointed out. "The Comanche hold them in scorn – and are please to make trouble for them."

James Shaw nodded in agreement. The discussions continued in a leisurely fashion for some hours – for that was the way of his people, but that was the same conclusion which everyone present agreed upon. Jim considered their mission to have been fulfilled, and Toby agreed.

"After all," remarked Jim to his blood-brother as they prepared for the long ride back to San Antonio to brief Captain Hays, "There is no actual proof presented that your people or any of the other settled tribes had anything to do with Balfour's claims, only Balfour's hot-headed accusations."

"Which too many people believe," Toby pointed out. "One of the teachers in the Moravian school used to say that a lie is halfway around the world while the truth is still putting on moccasins."

"At least, we can put the whole matter before Captain Hays, and he can put our findings to President Houston. This with the support of John Ford, which certainly should count for something."

John Ford, having fulfilled his own mission, was agreeable to traveling with them.

"Safer than riding alone," he remarked cheerily. Jim didn't mind – the man was stimulating company, and it turned out they had many mutual acquaintances and friends.

The good fellowship and feeling of accomplishment lasted until they came past the Balfour place and turned aside to pay their respects. Compared to their previous visit, there seemed to be a great gathering of people; horses in the corral, wagons and carts drawn up before the barn, and drawn up before the trading post. The garden, with the row of flowering shrubs, was set with trestle tables, at which people were dining. It was rather like the gathering at the Shaw settlement – only there was no evidence of gaiety or rejoicing. As they rode down the hill, they saw that the door to the house stood open. With a feeling of foreboding, Jim noted a garland of black fabric draped on it.

"I wonder what's up?" John Ford remarked. "It looks like they're holding a rally ... or a revival."

"I have no idea," Jim replied, "But let us find young Kinderhook. He should be somewhere about the trading post. He can tell us what's going on."

When they found Seth Kinderhook, looking unexpectedly somber in a dark coat and tall collar with an elaborate but inexpertly tied neckcloth, he looked at them in mild surprise.

"I guess you didn't hear," he said. "Ed – my brother-in-law... he died three days ago. The day after you-all passed by on your way to Fort Bird. We buried him this morning. Everyone from the county round came to the funeral. My sister and her friends laid on a good table, for everyone who came to show their respects."

"I'm sorry to hear that," Jim replied; he was shaken, but not as deeply as he might have been, if he had liked Ed Balfour more. "I know that he was ill. I didn't think that he was sick to death."

"I guess you would call it the bloody flux," Seth Kinderhook confided. "He couldn't keep nothing he ate or drank down, those last few days, not even the cordial that Sadie made special for him. If he weren't vomiting, he was sitting on the chamber pot. I 'spect that he was expecting it – kept saying that he saw halos in the light – the heavenly light leaking into this world, I guess."

"What will your sister do now?" Jim asked, while John Ford and Toby made sympathetic noises. Jim did notice out of the corner of his eye that John was looking fixedly at the row of roses and other shrubs. One of them had peculiar long narrow leaves – dark green and shaped like spear-points.

"Carry on here," Seth replied, proudly straightening his narrow shoulders. "She's got me to help her. This place is a good one, aside from the Comanche raiding when the fit takes them. But we'll do all right. We got friends and we got this place. No one's ever gonna drive us off it, not that I'm grown."

"Good fortune on you, and your sister," Jim said honestly. "Convey my condolences to your sister. We won't impose, since we want to get to Bastrop by nightfall."

"Thank you, sir," Seth bid them a distracted farewell. They weren't kin, after all, or particular friends to the Balfour clan, and rode on their way. Only John Ford turned in the saddle, and looked back, as they rode away.

"The bloody flux," he replied, when Jim asked him why. "It's … I was just wondering. So many ways of dying, in this world of ours. I don't want to think ill of a lady, but …"

"But – what?" Jim asked, while Toby snorted with suppressed amusement.

"That bush, the one with the yellow flowers? Did you notice it, especially?" John Ford replied. "Did you even recognize it?"

"No. I thought it was a peculiar kind of rose. It was planted with all the other roses," Jim replied.

John Ford heaved a deep sigh. "You're no botanist, Mr. Reade – certainly no gardener. That's a peculiar plant from South America – newly popular among ladies with gardens in Galveston and along the coast – ornamental, not requiring a lot of water, very pretty blooms ... and deadly poisonous. Everything about the oleander shrub is most deadly poison, every single thing – the blossoms, the leaves, the twigs and the wood. The symptoms of poisoning with oleander," John Ford added, with an oddly professorial air, "Include those which duplicate that of the bloody flux. Vomiting, diarrhea – and the delusion of seeing halos of light ..."

***

A week later, in Captain Hays' quarters in old San Antonio.

"Ah," Jack said, lighting his pipe with a spill touched on the coals in the tiny fireplace. It was spring, and still chilly in the evening after the sun went down. "You are plagued by the possibility that Ed Balfour might have been poisoned to death by his wife. But there were no complaints among his kin and no inquiry from the sheriff. Everyone seems to believe that he fell to a chronic illness."

"It's ... convenient," Jim stared into the fire, the hot glowing coals on the tiny corner hearth. "Too convenient. And that ... Mr. Shaw would say that it is not a rightness to things. An ill-spoken, venomous man, with unfounded grudges against practically everyone, including his wife. I mean – who could blame her, really, after being maliciously ill-treated by her husband. Perhaps she had good reason. Poison is a female weapon, after all. But still, it does not sit well with me, Jack. Murder – if it is murder, and there is no way that we can prove it as such – does not sit well with me. All of our problems, President Houston's, Mrs. Balfour's are all solved by a convenient death. The success of the peace conference at Bird's Fort, Edward Balfour's constant incitement against those Indians who are our allies. It goes against my sense of justice."

"You have an over-developed Puritan conscience, Jim," Jack puffed at his pipe, having gotten the tobacco in it to finally alight. "Take the comfort that you can, my stiletto-man. In the end, all are judged at St. Peter's gate into Heaven. If justice cannot be done here in the earthly realm – it will be done when we stand before Our Creator."

5 – The Fifth Adventure: Two Houses, Alike in Dignity

The message from Jack arrived by courier from Austin, where members of the Legislature were assembling, preparing to meet in session.

There is a problem brewing in Austin; yours and Mr. Shaw's problem-solving skills are required at once. Or sooner, if at all possible. A civil war must be averted. Your quarters are with me, as I have rented a house – signed, Jack Hays, Captain of Texas Rangers

PS – I will explain all upon your arrival. White house on hilltop east of capitol bldg.

"Our commander orders, and we should pack our traps." Jim set aside the note, and wondered what their commander could possibly mean by this cryptic communication. There was an unmentioned addendum to this – there always was, and it seemed to them both that Jack Hays derived enormous amusement from saving it to the last moment before he sent them off to deal with the situation. "We should set off first thing in the morning – it's a two-day ride, at least, and I don't want to kill our horses or ourselves by traveling at night. I wonder what on earth Jack means by a civil war?"

"We shall find out when we reach Austin," Toby replied, tranquilly.

Four mornings later, the two of them rode down the track that led to the erstwhile capital of Texas – the scratch-made shanty-town set among tall trees, which once had been Waterloo-on-the-Colorado. But ever since Mirabeau Lamar

153

had shot a buffalo in what would be a main town intersection and fallen in love with the epic beauty of the wooded glades, mountains and silver river – the place had become Austin, the final capital city of Texas, the place where the Legislature met, and the archives of the nation were stored – for all that Sam Houston could do about it. It was common knowledge that President Houston, the hero of San Jacinto, disliked the fact that Austin was so far out on the frontier, so close to the hunting grounds of the Comanche and so far from the settled portions of Texas. But those who had cast in their lot and fortunes with establishing a town in the very heart and center of what was claimed to be the whole of Texas – they were a doughty and stubborn lot.

"Where is Captain Jack staying?" Toby asked, as they approached the ramble of frame buildings, scattered throughout the valley below. The largest of them was a well-fortified ramble, centered around a log cabin raised on tall stilts, which looked as if it were trying to run away from the ramshackle outbuildings surrounding it.

"Jack said that for the term of the Legislature, he was renting rooms from the Archbishop of Texas, who is never there, but ever out on the road tending to his flock," Jim replied. "The Archbishop has obtained freehold of a small but exquisite residence with many modern conveniences. I think that it must be that small white house, on the hill above the river."

It was indeed a charming small house in a pretty situation, with a deep porch across the front, the porch roof held up by six pairs of slender white pillars, above a garden set about with several shady trees. Their weary horses climbed last quarter mile of dusty track as the setting sun turned the deep-running waters of the river below to a reach of shining silver. Jack, as they had half-expected, waited for them on that porch, his pipe already sending up a thread of smoke.

"Oh, good – you're here," he remarked. "I thought you would be. I told M. de Pleuyette to lay two more places on the table for supper, against your arrival. We're dining here – in more or less privacy, so that I may let you both in as to the lay of the land."

"Oh, good," Jim replied. He was not relishing facing the scrum of dining at one of Austin's inns and boarding houses when the Legislature was in session, not until he and Toby had been fully briefed as to the nature of what Jack had termed a civil war. "Do we have time to wash up, and unroll our blankets?"

"None of that, with pallets on the floor," Jack replied with an airy gesture toward the front door. "The first door to the right it has some proper bedsteads in it. I demand first-class quarters for my stiletto-men, you know."

"I'll remember that the next time I'm sleeping under a mesquite bush in the Llano," Jim replied, with a nod toward his blood-brother. "I assume the stable and corral is around this way? Let us see to the horses, and then we'll come around. I want to hear the whole story, Jack – even before we set down to supper."

"Of course." Jack knocked the spent tobacco out of his pipe, and grinned – a very boyish and mischievous grin.

"You'll enjoy this one, Jim' I promise you will. A civilized little civil war over the teacups and supper trenchers."

"That's what I was afraid of," Jim replied.

Half an hour later, when the horses had been settled in a stall in what turned out to be a commodious and welcoming stable, Jim and Toby joined Jack on the porch of the Archbishop's very modern house. The western sky, beyond the vista of many-slanted roofs clustering around what was intended to be a grand avenue pointing toward the capital building, had gone to shades of orange and purple, attending on the sun setting in splendor. The river, with light fleeing from the sky, was the dull color of lead. There were several comfortable chairs arrayed along the verandah. The odor of good cooking floating on the light evening breeze from the summer kitchen around in back proved to be a mouth-watering distraction. Jim settled into the first of those chairs, and watched the first golden lights begin blooming in windows down below.

"Well?" Jim hinted gently, and Jack looked out to the town below, with a sigh.

"You recall your Shakespeare, hoss – for I know that you are an educated man. *Two households, both alike in dignity (In fair Verona, where we lay our scene), From ancient grudge break to new mutiny* ... alas, it has come to that, in Fair Austin, where we lay our new scene, or at least, our two dignified houses have broken to new mutiny... although, how old the grudge might be, is a matter of conjecture."

"You are going to explain this, eventually," Jim hinted again, with his own sigh. Their commander, who held the responsibility for security in a quarrelsome nation beset with vengeful enemies on either side had a peculiar sense of humor.

"I shall, Jim, and on this very moment. I am certain that you noted the establishment of Bullock's Hotel, as you approached our capital city ... that block-long sprawl of buildings at Congress Avenue and Pecan? Yes, Bullock is one of the stalwart citizens of Austin, and his establishment is one of the most long-term. Indeed, in times of trouble, his place was the fort to which all took refuge. Well, half the Legislature is quartered there, although the work of the cooks in his kitchen is ... well, barely edible. But his pork sausage and smoked bacon almost make up for that lack. He keeps a herd of pigs, you know. Those pigs are responsible for me having the rent of this estimable bit of property, I'll have you know – but that is another story, entirely."

"You should tell it to me, some time," Jim replied. "But not until it is irrelevant to our mission – the mission that you have summoned us for."

"Indeed," Jack replied, with a deprecative chuckle. "Now – the other half of the Legislature, and President Houston is staying at Eberly House, just across Congress Avenue from Bullock's Hotel. That establishment is owned by Mrs. Angelina Eberly - a widow of estimable character, and considerable determination, also a stubborn and long-term resident of Austin. Her place has long been favored by President Houston. But for some unfathomable reason, Mrs.

Eberly and Mr. Bullock are engaged in a vicious feud against each other and their respective customers are in danger of being drawn into it! That, on top of every other faction and feud in Texas! There are no other hotels or boarding houses as notable as these two – oh, there is a house on the hill above the river at the edge of town, owned by another widow who takes in select roomers. And farther down Congress Avenue, a small boarding house with only two or three rooms, run by a Mr. and Mrs. Armstead ... but they offer neither the comfort and fine table of Mrs. Eberly's, or the lively company afforded by Bullock also keeping a generous tavern. There are times, Jim, that one can hear the ruction in his taproom all the way here."

"A lively discussion of politics, well-lubricated," Jim agreed. "Now I see your wisdom in staying in the Archbishop's house. You can uphold some pretense of being neutral."

"Above it all," Jack agreed. "And M. Pleuyette's cooking is every bit as good as the table that Mrs. Eberly sets. If you and Shaw can begin your investigations tomorrow, I have every hope of resolving this sad situation. There's an air to the whole thing that I do not like – if I were a suspicious man, I might come to believe that someone is inflaming the situation for their own ends."

With these last words in mind, Jim and Toby consulted long over the breakfast table – a long table spread in the wide hallway, which ran from back to front of the Archbishop's residence. The double doors at either end stood open, enticing the pleasant morning breeze to wander through the length of the building. Mr. Pleuyette proved to be an agreeable Frenchman, whose' English was fluent, yet strongly flavored with the accent of his native land. He served as caretaker for the property when the Archbishop was away tending to his far-flung flock, and cook and housekeeper when the Archbishop or his tenants were in residence.

"I 'ave been here since the beginning," that worthy had announced, upon bringing in the tray with the covered salvers of scrambled egg, bacon, chops, sausages, baked biscuits and toast stacked upon it. "I was here when the Comte de Dubois de Saligny had cause to build this house, as a representative of our *belle France*. I know of all in this town of Austin, for I was here almost at the beginning, when the pigs ran in the streets and bats flew in and out of the windows of the capital building!"

"It is curious," Jim mused, through a mouthful of buttered toast, "That Mrs. Eberly and Mr. Bullock have long been doing business in Austin; this innkeeping/boarding house enterprise, without any whisper of dissention between them, until this present day. They are both founding citizens of the town, ever since President Lamar established it as the capital city. I wonder if you might be correct, in his suspicion of someone deliberately inciting a feud."

"It has a definite touch of a female hand," Jack agreed.

"When women take to the warpath," Toby nodded, somberly, "They take no prisoners – for they war without mercy, since everything, including the life under their own heartbeat, that of their children – may be at stake."

"Aye," Jack helped himself to another beautifully spiced and grilled breakfast chop. "Hasn't it always been told among the Tribes, that the women are the most inventive and cruel when it comes to torturing enemy captives ..."

"It is the Way," Toby was applying himself to his own chop. "My mother has always said that the ways of life in the wild tribes like the Comanche are so cruel, that the women of them find a kind of pleasure and release in tormenting any enemy that has the misfortune to fall into their hands – because they otherwise might wish to torture their fathers, brothers, and husbands."

"My God!" Jim exclaimed. It did make a kind of horrid sense. He finished his toast, slathered with a spoonful of English orange marmalade. Yes, the Archbishop's pantry afforded all kinds of luxuries – and contemplated the matter at hand. He had no doubt that women, with so few weapons to hand, as men commonly did, could be sneaky and vicious in defending what was theirs. "I wonder if our own could be ... yes, upon consideration, they could be. My own mother has reported many a delicate slander over the teacups, and I suppose that Mrs. Shaw could say the same."

"She could," Toby agreed, over a mouthful of chop and crisp toast. "So, what is our course of investigation, Brother?"

Jim considered. "I suggest that Mrs. Eberly should be the first of those that we should call upon, this morning – and perhaps treat with Mr. Bullock later in the day."

"Excellent notion, hoss," Jack agreed. "Mrs. Eberly conducts a well-ordered and home-like house, whereas Mr. Bullock's guests are more addicted to late-night revels."

"Any other relevant observations about the two establishments that you have noted? I presume that with so many guests that there must be hired staff at both places."

"There is, most certainly," Jack helped himself to more coffee. "Mrs. Eberly has half a dozen hired girls to do the laundry, wait on table, sweep and dust – mostly daughters of families in Austin, although her cook is a free black woman from Richmond. She does have several hired men who do the outdoor and the heavy work – cutting wood, hauling water. Mr. Bullock has likewise, although Mrs. Bullock and their daughters do the cooking. Most of the folk who work at Bullock's are kin in some degree, although there are a few more hired just for the extra work with the Legislature in session."

"So a fair number of people, in and out of both places, on an average day." Jim thought that he had better unlimber his note-taking hand. "And what kind of accusations have been flying back and forth, as part of the animus between the two?"

"That," Jack said, with a sigh, "Is for the pair of you to investigate. I didn't want to muddy your investigation by seeming to take too much interest in the specifics and appearing to take sides. I just nodded, expressed my sympathies, and promised that my best stiletto-men would be along, presently."

"Grateful for the appreciation," Jim observed, wryly. "We'll do our best. At least, neither party has inspired any dead bodies, like that feud between the Taylors and the Sutton's down in La Vernia a few years ago."

"Yet," said, Jack, depressingly.

161

Jim and Toby washed up after breakfast, taking special care to put on their cleanest and most respectable clothes, those coats, trousers, shirts, and cravats reserved for when they had to appear in good and prosperous company – not in the rough gear and hunting coats worn on the trail. They were both painfully aware that it was likely they would encounter many notable citizens of Texas in the course of this mission – and that as such, the nation of Texas was their employer. Jim took good care to tuck a small notebook, a pen and inkbottle into his coat pocket. He and Toby walked down the hill upon which the Archbishop's residence overlooked the bustling little town, and directed their steps to the main thoroughfare – Congress Avenue, which slashed a straight way from the riverbank to the hill on which the rambling house within a crude palisade of logs served as the Capitol building.

"It has not a patch on the Houses of Parliament in Westminster where the government of Britain meets, or even the US Capitol building, with a noble colonnade and dome," Jim confessed. "Indeed – it looks like the outhouse to either of those. I hope that eventually we will have a nobler structure…"

"It suits," Toby replied. "For our elected leaders meet only once every two years, and every man holding office has need to practice their trade in between times … otherwise, if we build a palace for them to work in, they might begin to assume great airs for themselves, thinking that they are princes and nobles of old, and all the rest should scrape and bow ... at least, this way, a man might come before his chiefs and war-leaders and treat with them as brothers."

"But for the honor of the nation," Jim ventured and then considered that Toby might have a valid point. They turned their steps toward the Eberly House – a comfortable and compact place, wrought of carpentered planks, and white-washed. The shutters which were folded flat against the white walls were painted rust-red, and the brass doorknob on the main entry was polished as highly as if it were gold. The door on which it was mounted opened almost at once to Jim's firm rap upon it.

"If you're looking for a place to stay," announced the young lady who appeared in the doorway, "Miz Eberly said to tell you that we are full-up. There ain't even a place to spread out a pallet on the parlor floor..."

"We do not seek a place to stay," Jim replied, doffing his hat. "We are already accommodated, in that respect. Would you be so kind as to announce us to Mrs. Eberly? I am James Reade, of the State Rangers, and this is my associate, Mr. Shaw of the Delaware. Captain Hays has sent us on a matter of some import to Mrs. Eberly."

"I'll see if she is free," the girl replied, with a somewhat uncertain air. "If you would follow me to the parlor... she's always awful busy on Wednesdays, since that is baking day, an' tomorrow is ironing ..."

"Thank you," Jim replied, and the girl closed the door after herself. Jim stood on the hearthrug, surveying Mrs. Eberly's immaculate parlor – a plain but comfortable room, adorned with a few pieces of upholstered furniture plainly imported from the East, a wood-framed fireplace and overmantel of local work, adorned with china, framed prints and waxworks under glass – likewise imported from the East. A rug of braided rags covered the floor between upholstered chairs and those with plain rush-woven seats; a home-made rug of outworn rags, but in pleasing colors. A fine wood and brass-trimmed clock ticked away, on the fireplace mantel. Jim and Toby exchanged meaningful glances – they both had made their own, yet congruent estimations of the estimable lady's household. Comfortable, well-organized, reaching beyond what was normally the standard for a household on the far frontier. No wonder that President Houston favored her hospitality, when the Legislature met in Austin on the Colorado.

After a wait of some five minutes, measured by the ticking of the clock and the slow movement of the larger hand, they heard the girl's voice in the hallway outside; too low to hear exactly what was said, but the louder woman's imperious voice came quite clearly through the closed door.

"I'm certain that the matter will not take long, Kitty, even if it is as important as the gentlemen claim – not when I have so much to do." The door opened, and the owner of the voice appeared in the doorway; a stout and white-haired older lady clad in a black dress with unfashionably narrow skirts, who was just then handing her work apron to Kitty. "Well, then – Ranger Reade? I trust you will be brief, for as you may imagine, we are very busy, what with the Legislature meeting and all."

"Madame Eberly!" Jim bowed, courteously. "I will mince no words; Captain Hays has tasked me with resolving the ... particular disagreement between your good self and Mr. Bullock."

"Well, I'm glad to hear that!" the redoubtable landlady replied, settling herself into the largest chair with a flounce of her black skirts. "Take a pew, then, you and your partner – I won't mince any words, but it's about time someone took an interest! It's a mortal shame in this world that such calumnies – such horrid slanders can be heaped upon an honest, respectable woman! I wouldn't have credited Richard Bullock with being so spiteful, telling such lies, not after all the years we've been in the same line o' business as we are..."

"Can you give me an example of what Mr. Bullock has said, which you believe to be a lie?" Jim cut into the spate of her remarks, rather in the spirit of someone stepping into a gushing stream, not knowing how deep the water or how powerful the current might be.

Mrs. Eberly fluffed up like an angry hen. "Just a week, ten days ago it was – one of my boarders got sick, vomiting into one o' them spittoons in the house chamber he was – and within the hour, Mr. Bullock was putting it around to his household, and his boarders that it was our cooking that done it! Poisoning our lodgers, he said! There ought to be an investigation, he said! Imagine the cheek – an' then I had to comfort Persephony, she was that distraught! I had to practically double her wages to keep her from quitting on the spot and going back to Richmond! Persephony, I said – everyone et of your cooking that night before, and none of us was vomiting – and if you asked me plain, Mr. Robinson was vomiting because of overindulging with that rot-gut panther-pee that Mr. Bullock serves to customers in that sink of iniquity and drunkenness of his!" The Widow Eberly settled her skirts with an angry flounce and continued. "Then there are all them drunks who come across the Avenue, knocking at the door at all hours, saying they want to spark with my girls! They've got it into their heads somehow that I'm running a house of ill-repute! Where could they be getting that notion, but in Mr. Bullock's taproom! And me a respectable widow, running a respectable boarding house, I ask you!"

"That must be extraordinarily awkward for you, Mrs. Eberly," Jim said, carefully not meeting Toby's eye, knowing that his blood-brother would be much amused. "Do you have any idea which of Mr. Bullock's people could be suggesting that to his customers?"

"I don't want to tell you no lies," Mrs. Eberly replied, with an indignant sniff. "But I think it's that wretched Joe McConnel, who runs the taproom most evenings ... him with an evil tongue in a handsome face. I wouldn't put it past him – and that Mr. Bullock would encourage him out of spite."

Jim retrieved his notebook, pen and inkbottle from his coat pocket. With a sigh, he dipped the pen into ink, saying, "If you would be so kind – tell us of any other ... calumnies that have been leveled against you and your enterprise by Mr. Bullock and his party ..."

"You might need another notebook!" Mrs. Eberly exclaimed, and Jim saw out of the corner of his eye that Toby was trying to hide his amusement. Some twenty minutes later, with almost every page of the notebook filled – and on both sides – Mrs. Eberly personally saw them both to the door. When it closed behind them, they walked for a little way toward the capitol building.

"Well ..." Toby mused. "That certainly allowed the Widow Eberly to unburden herself. What a list!"

"Spite and nasty rumors," Jim agreed. "But there's enough of them, beginning a few months ago to hint that there is some other impulse besides mere business rivalry at work. After all, both Bullock's Hotel and Eberly House have always agreeably split up what guests seeking rooms that existed previously. It makes one begin to wonder what changed in recent months to set them at each other."

"I'm glad that you thought of making a list of Mrs. Eberly's hired folk, and all of her guests," Toby remarked. "Perhaps Captain Jack may see something significant – some connection. As I track game and horses in the wild, he tracks human folk in your civilized lands."

"Perhaps," Jim agreed. He squinted at the sun, now sailing in a pure cerulean sky overhead – well past noon. "I think we should go and get Mr. Bullock's side of the story. See what he says, and make a list of his hired folk and his guests as well – the regular ones, not the ones who come to drink at his tavern only now and again..." It had been his experience that the mere fact of making lists and meditating on them sometimes brought about illumination, an insight which led to a resolution of the matter in question.

Bullock's Hotel was a crowded place at midday, what with the meals being served in the hotel dining room – this was a clap-board sided hall constructed by walling in a square log cabin raised on tall log piers. The whole building looked as if it wanted to run away on gangling legs. Jim paused in the doorway, about to ask where Mr. Bullock could be found. The room was packed with men, seated elbow-to-elbow at long tables, while a few young women and a single lad in a grubby apron wended their way between them, burdened with trays of full serving dishes – sausages sizzling with fat, baked beans swimming in their own savory liquor, boiled greens, platters of sliced pork roast ... the odor of food, and of too many human bodies all crammed together was almost too much for Jim's senses, being that he had not eaten since breakfast in the Archbishop's house many hours before.

"Where can we find Mr. Bullock?" he called to the nearest servitor – the lad in the grubby apron.

"In the taproom, I think!" the lad replied, with a jerk of his chin in the direction of the main sprawl of the Bullock establishment. Jim and Toby ventured through the main doors – the taproom was even more jammed than the dining room. Too obviously, many of Bullock's guests preferred to drink their noon repast.

But Bullock was not there, although Jim, by dint of working his elbows, fought through the crowd to the bar, which was secured by a set of sturdy grills in the old-fashioned way of the century before. The barkeep cocked an ear toward Jim's shouted query, and replied,

"Round in back, I think – trouble at the smokehouse!"

The smokehouse at Bullocks sat a little distance from the main buildings, and readily identified by aromatic gray smoke leaking from every crack and cranny of the ramshackle log structure. Those buildings which lined Congress Avenue and gave at first glance the impression of a well-settled town raveled out to corrals, gardens and plowed fields within two or three hundred yards, and the area behind Bullock's was no exception, augmented by a muddy pond in which snored several large and dirty pigs.

Richard Bullock somewhat resembled one of his own hogs, being large, black-haired, hulking of shoulder, muddy about the boots and trouser legs, and displaying a countenance which now wore a threatening expression – rather like the nearest pig, glowering at Jim over a pile of fresh potato peelings.

"Thanks, but I already ate," Jim told the pig, who grunted sullenly and wandered away. "Mr. Bullock – can I have a word?" he raised his voice, and Bullock, who was already in mid-tirade, shouting at two of his shrinking underlings.

"If you've a mind to," Richard Bullock growled. "Who the hell are you and what do you want."

"A word with you, first of all," Jim introduced himself and explained his mission and authority yet once again. "Aye, then – if Captain Hays sent you. Good. Come to the china parlor – we can talk privately there. You!" he shot over his shoulder to the hired men. "The meat in this batch is spoiled, for certain. Scour everything inside with vinegar and shovel out the dirt below and set a new fire with fresh wood to burn before we set more to process – Throw this batch to the pigs, since we can hardly feed it to the guests, then!"

"Wouldn't that be a bit like cannibalism, then – feeding pork and sausages to your pigs?" Jim ventured, as he and Toby followed the lord of Bullock's Hotel around to the back door of the sprawling compound.

Richard Bullock grunted – very much like one of his pigs. "Aye, well – the beasts would eat a man and crunch the bones, soon enough, given the chance."

"So ... what has happened to this batch in your smokehouse, that you must throw away everything and start anew."

"Sabotage of the meat in my smokehouse!" Richard Bullock snarled. "Someone – and I have a very good idea of the evil crone to caused it – poured piss all over the wood! And the batch is ruined, ruined beyond fixing? Who wants to eat sausages and roasts that taste like the inside of a burned chamberpot? No one – and this with the first meeting of the Legislature in years! I'll throttle that scrawny witch, I swear I will!"

"You cannot prove that Mrs. Eberly is behind this, surely?" Jim didn't think that he could dampen the man's fury, but at least he could try. Mr. Bullock flung open the nearest gate into the hotel grounds with a crash that shivered the whole fence.

"Who else, but the only other substantial boarding house in Austin?!" Mr. Bullock roared. "There are only the two of us in competition – the Armstead's place hardly counts, and the woman who owns the house on the hill outside of town only rents rooms to her lah-de-dah husband's old friends!"

"It's come to my mind that such might not be the case, precisely," Jim said, carefully, as soon as he and Toby had been admitted to that room in the Bullock Hotel which seemed to be a private family parlor – a simple, pleasant room with a single high window. A series of nicely-fitted shelves held a collection of pretty china plates, cups and a tea service; items obviously cherished by Mrs. Bullock and too fine and fragile to use for hotel guests. There was also a small piano in the corner, which surprised Jim very much.

"It's the only one in Austin," Mr. Bullock explained, rather proudly. "My Mary – Mrs. Bullock, she plays it for her friends and when we have a proper meeting of the Presbyterian fellowship."

"Quite the cultured salon," Jim murmured, and Mr. Bullock's heavy countenance brightened.

"We may not be in the thick of commerce like them in Galveston, or Richmond, or in old Stephen Austin's colony, where most Texans live – but we get by. We have great hopes for this place, so we do, even out here on the far frontier. Never forget what President Lamar said – this-here Austin is the very center of all of Texas. Now," he bent a shrewd look upon Jim. "You and this Injun pal of yours – you say that Captain Hays sent you; that he thinks there is something fishy goin' on between me an' Miz Eberly."

"We do ... he does." Jim explained his and Jack's thinking to him, and it seemed that he could see the gears of Mr. Bullock's thoughts turning slowly and ponderously, possibly with a slight creaking as he considered that possibility.

"Well, Cap'n Hays, he's a man of parts," Mr. Bullock finally admitted. "No flies on him when it comes to matters of concern to the nation. An' from what I hear tell, you two are some of his sharpest fellows. You're Dan'l Reade's brother, ain't you? Dan'l Reade from Bastrop? Thought so; a fine man, a good fighter. Rode with him, now and again, when the militia was called out."

Jim felt the catch of grief at his throat, the familiar old grief at the death of his brother by treachery at the hands of the murdering traitor Gallantin ... so many men in Texas knew Daniel Reade and thought well of him. With an effort, he turned his own mind back to the matter at hand. He took out pen, notebook, and inkbottle, setting them on a handy little table.

"Now tell me," Jim assumed his post professorial air. "Of all the various instances of harmful acts which you have blamed Mrs. Eberly for ... occurrences which were not mere chance but deliberate ... such as the ruination of your smokehouse, just now. And for how long do you believe this has been happening?"

"About a year, give or take," Richard Bullock scowled, but not so much in anger, as in the effort to recall. "It's driven my poor Mary nearly to distraction – it's almost as if some bad, malicious spirit has moved into our place and called down every scrap of bad luck imaginable."

It turned out to be a long list – almost as long as the Widow Eberly's catalog. Laundry hung out to dry being smutted while on an unattended clothesline – that had happened several times, to the fury of Mrs. Bullock and the hired girls who had labored over tubs and scrub-boards for hours, only to have their work be for naught. Baskets of potatoes and yams brought from the root cellar revealed to be half-rotted, and slimy upon being brought to the kitchen, a baking of bread ruined through someone adding too much salt to the dough set for rising ... hired men suddenly not available for urgent work when the Bullocks had assumed that they would. It all had a familiar feel – akin to the various small household disasters which had overtaken the Eberly House and rattled the management thereof. At the end of the recitation, Jim asked for a list of those who had been employed at Bullocks' Hotel, thanked Mr. Bullock for his time, and looked toward Toby, who had been sitting impassively in the corner, listening to Jim's questions and Mr. Bullock's extensive reply.

"Can you think of anything that we might have missed, Mr. Shaw?"

Toby shook his head – no. When it came to interrogations of this sort, he usually chose to efface himself and watch, testing every word, expression, flicker of doubt on a countenance. Mr. Bullock generously offered to stand them a drink in the taproom – he seemed a great deal more cordial now than he had when they first approached him – which Jim refused, explaining their need to avoid partiality, and the late hour. It was already late in the afternoon, with shadows stretching long across Congress Avenue, when Jim and Toby climbed up the steep hill to where the Archbishop's house waited under the sheltering oak trees. Halfway there, a young girl with a basket over her arm came running after them, breathlessly calling their names – the same girl who had admitted them to Mrs. Eberly's place that very morning.

They waited for her to catch up, which she did, pink-cheeked and panting.

"Mr. Reade, Mr. Shaw! Ma made some little sugared cakes for your supper tonight, or for breakfast tomorrow, if you like. Mrs. Eberly sends her regards, too – and she said ..." the girl paused to recover her breath, "If there is anything more she can tell you, you have only to ask."

"Thank you ..." Jim fished in his memory for the girl's name, among all the others that he had taken note of in a single day.

"Kitty," the girl flashed a smile, under the brim of her sunbonnet. "Catherine Barlow."

"Thank you, Kitty," Jim accepted the basket. "And thank your mother, Mrs. Barlow for her generosity,"

"Oh, Ma is Mrs. Armstead," Kitty replied, with a blush. "Mr. Armstead is my stepfather."

"And a fortunate man, to wed with a good cook," Jim replied without thinking, His own mother was an ambitious, but awful cook, her own opinion to the contrary. Kitty blushed deeper and giggled at the compliment, bobbed a brief curtsy, and took herself down the path again.

"Armstead," Toby mused as the two continued up the hill, Jim wishing very much that he had accepted Mr. Bullock's offer of a drink – for the afternoon was quite warm, although it was late in the year, and certain of the trees were already touched with gold. "Did not Jack mention that a Mr. and Mrs. Armstead also kept a boarding house – a very small one, hardly worth mentioning, when in competition with Bullock and Eberly?"

"So he did," Jim replied, "I guess they did better to hire out their daughter to Mrs. Eberly, so at least the girl could earn a wage while the Legislature was in session. I gather that Austin has been pretty much deserted, otherwise."

"It would be my thought, my brother," Toby ventured, "That someone whom they each have taken into their household, might not be entirely worthy of trust."

"Hmm," Jim replied, for he had privately begun to wonder also. That Bullock and Eberly both had been on good terms until recent months ... argued that a closer look might reward such suspicions. They spoke little, until they joined Jack, at ease on the verandah of the house, enjoying a pipe and cool drink, as the heat of the day abated somewhat.

"You have finished with your investigations?" Jack drawled, with gentle sarcasm.

"We wish," Jim replied. He drew inkbottle, pen and notebook out of his coat pocket, shedding that garment as well, relishing the momentary relief as the evening breeze fanned him, drying out his sweat-sodden shirt. "We spent the day interviewing Widow Eberly and Mr. Richard Bullock, accumulating a list of the outrages each insists that the other has inflicted upon them over the last six months or so, and the names of all their employees. Mr. Shaw has wondered if someone among those hired to assist with the rush of guests expected when the Legislature met might be causing malicious havoc among their respective households." Jim opened his notebook, to the pages which listed the respective employees of Bullock's Hotel and Eberly House. "Are any of these names familiar to you, Jack?"

Jack shook his head. "I know nothing of these Austin folk, save those men who might have ridden with me as Rangers, now and again. There's nothing that I know ... but save us – Mr. Pleuyette! He boasts of knowing everyone in Austin, from the earliest days – and he was here from the very first!" Jack turned and bellowed, in his command voice, "Pleuyette! *Attendez-moi*! We have need of your knowledge!"

In a moment, the Frenchman appeared from around the side of the house, still wearing his apron – the corner of it buttoned to his waistcoat and a shabby white cap on his head. He had a turning fork in his hand.

"M'sieu, the roast is nearly ready! What do you require, then?"

"Your undoubted intelligence as to a list of suspects," Jack replied, tersely. "Go and turn your roasts, put the sauces on the back to keep warm, attend to this list of names, and tell us what you know of them."

Mr. Pleuyette assented with a grunt, and no hint of surprise on his face. Jim began reading off the names, one by one. Mr. Pleuyette listened to each, looking into the distance, as he accounted for each one.

"... youngest daughter – her parents have a *petite ferme* two or three miles distant. She came to work in the household of Madame Eberly at the time of *le Noel* ... Mademoiselle Irene Gericault – she is an orphan, referred to Madame

Eberly and vouched for by his Excellence Archbishop Odin ... Mademoiselle Catherine Barlow is the daughter of Madame Armstead by her late husband, who has been working at Madame Eberly's auberge for five months ..."

"You have the most exact recall for the particulars of every young lady, Pleuyette," Jack remarked, with a wry grin. Mr. Pleuyette did not smile but remained entirely in earnest.

"*Mais certainement* – there are so very few demoiselles of marriageable age in Austin – each one is a notable pearl in the eyes of a gentleman deciding among them which will honor him with her hand..."

"That is the last of Widow Eberly's employees," Jim remarked – all had been accounted for; Miss Kitty Barlow was the most recent addition to the household. "Now for those in Mr. Bullock's employ – a groom and hostler, Augustus Toepperwein..."

"For two years," Mr. Pleuyette affirmed. "An immigrant from the Duchy of Saxe-Altenburg; his sister is also employed by Mrs. Bullock, to assist in the dining room."

Most of Bullock's employees were male, most the kind of wandering young men without family connections anywhere west of the Sabine. Of them, Mr. Pleuyette knew nothing to arouse suspicion until Jim came to the last one on the list. "Mr. Joseph McConnel – he has been here with his family for a year or so, man of all work when not tending bar in the taproom. He is a half-brother of M'sieu Armstead and came to work for M'sieu Bullock in the last six months."

"What an interesting coincidence," Jim mused. "I feel a certain prickling in my thumbs. That two people with close familial connections to the Armsteads – who must hope to rival Bullock and Eberly, in the provision of hospitality – are, within the last five or six months, employed by each business. Jack; this feud, accelerated by what is obviously sabotage within each house – has been going on for how long?"

"About six months, according to your lists," Jack, from the dawning expression on his own face, apparently was feeling the same prickling. "So, what better means might an upstart and struggling boarding house in a town like Austin take, then ruin their better-established rivals. Cut them down to size, wreck their standing with customers ... and better yet, get them to destroy each other. It's ... diabolical, Jim – diabolical!"

"Alas, we have no hard proof of such a scheme," Jim sighed. "Although I am certain in my heart that such is the case! We have suspicious coincidences – but no solid proof which would stand up before a judge in a court of law."

"We cannot do nothing," Toby pointed out, his dark eyes going between his brother and his chief. "It is ... an unbalancing of things, to allow such malice to continue without speaking."

"And if left to continue, it would embroil the whole town, for no reason than one family getting greedy," Jack agreed. "No, we can't ignore the situation. I can drop a quiet hint to the Armsteads – that we have a suspicion of what has been going on, and if they are wise enough ... take a hint and desist from such plotting."

"And I can speak to both Bullock and the Widow Eberly," Jim agreed. "Putting them wise to what we suspect."

"Tomorrow?" Jim closed his notebook with a sense of satisfaction – a quandary and mystery solved in a single day! That must set a new record."

* * *

Exactly a day later, Jim and Toby met with Jack, on the verandah of the Archbishop's house. All three wore expressions of contented triumph.

"How did it go, with Bullock and the Widow Eberly?" Jack lit his pipe and blew out a thin gray trickle of smoke, which dissipated nearly at once, under the wayward evening breeze. "Can you report that the feud is resolved, completely?"

"Absolutely, Captain," Jim replied. "I called on both to meet with me just this afternoon – on neutral ground of my choosing. This house, as a matter of fact. Mr. Pleuyette served tea and a nice little assortment of cakes ... Mrs. Eberly requested the recipe from him, as a matter of fact."

"How did the meeting go? I do not see any blood or bullet-holes," Jack grinned a little, to take the sting away. "So I presume that it went well."

"They were both a little suspicious at first," Jim related. "But as I outlined our theory, and built the case for deliberate fomenting of bad feelings based on deliberate sabotage ... the two of them began to see my point and agree..."

"Well, neither of them are stupid folk," Jack nodded. "And they have been in business long enough to have encountered all sorts."

"And they apologized handsomely for all the ill words directed at each other over the last few months – recollected at length how long they had been friends and fellow citizens when practically everyone else abandoned Austin because of the danger from Comanche raids. It was quite touching," Jim reported, with abundant satisfaction. "I am pretty certain the feud between them is old news; they both acknowledged how easily they had been fooled by people they trusted... and speaking of which, how did your little visit with the Armsteads go?"

"Satisfactorily," Jack looked exceedingly smug. "In accordance with your advice regarding the laws of slander and on the chance that Mr. Armstead would take offense and challenge me to a duel were I completely frank, I made no direct accusation. I merely noted the interesting coincidence that unfortunate accidents at Bullocks' Hotel and Eberly House began happening right about the time that Mr. Armstead's half-brother and Mrs. Armstead's daughter began working at those places. Plus, the sudden appearance of insinuations that Mr. Bullock and Mrs. Eberly were responsible ... when each of those parties had been on the most amenable terms before."

"A nice line in insinuations, yourself, Captain," Jim allowed. Jack showed a wolfish grin.

"Yes, wasn't it. I also suggested ... in the most tactful manner imaginable – that the Armstead welcome in Austin would turn decidedly cold if everyone among the long-time residents learned how the source of all those nasty, nasty rumors came about, deliberately and as a campaign to ruin their respective prosperous businesses. Mr. Bullock and Mrs. Eberly came to Austin early on the town's foundation, stuck it out through all the bad times, provided a refuge when the Comanche threatened to wipe out the town ... and," Jack showed his teeth in a feral, merciless grin. "I suggested, in the most tactful manner imaginable – that it would not be advantageous to them to have it known among the old residents of Austin that they had colluded in attempting to ruin such long-time, respectable citizens in furthering their own advantages. That was all that I needed to say. Both Mr. and Mrs. Armstead both turned as pale as bleached linen, and assured me, solo and in chorus, that of course they had no such intention, and it was only wicked tongues clattering ... and so, I think this matter has been settled," Jack added with an air of satisfaction. "Would that all such conflicts could be settled so decisively! I will keep an attentive eye on the situation ... which is just as well, for the daily mail brings me notice of another situation, in which I may need the skills of my best stiletto-men."

"Where?" Jim fetched up a deep sigh from the very depths of his being. He had enjoyed the brief days in Austin, and especially the comfort of the Archbishop's house and M. Pleuyette's excellent cooking.

"You'll never guess," Jack grinned. "And you'll love it. To Washington in the United States ... as special couriers, on an errand of state."

Notes – Lone Star Blood

The First Adventure – The Matter of Jedidiah

This adventure is built entirely from my imagination – there is no plantation near Richmond, Texas, named Pecan Grove, which was inherited, on paper by a tame macaw; if there is, it is entirely coincidental. The matter of chattel slavery, or "the peculiar institution" as it was termed in popular contemporary parlance, had a number of oddities and anomalies which I have hinted at in this story – including the fact that a slave might be safer and more secure in their person, than a free person of color walking about the streets at the time. This is not to make a case for slavery – but to point up some of the very curious oddities. Those people who existed at that time and in those places in the US where chattel slavery was permitted had to make accommodation with the practice as their circumstances and consciences dictated – not necessarily as those of us in the present would have wished.

The Second Adventure – The King of Kibera

This story – which any reasonably well-read reader or movie aficionado will immediately recognize as having the same plot as Rudyard Kipling's short story and the 1975 movie made from it; *The Man Who Would Be King*, with Michael Caine and Sean Connery. It's a perfectly riveting story, and I've been a fan of Kipling since I could read books with long words in them. I wondered how well it would translate to an American setting, in the southwest, with a secretive Indian tribe dwelling in the cliffs and mesas, and as one of my writing friends remarked – every excellent plot ought to be given a chance to romp in any other geographic location which could accommodate it. The names of Sir Alexander Connaway and Richard Coign-Gordon are also a nod to the actors Connery and Caine. The character of Sir Alexander as written here was partly inspired by the character of the 19th century soldier, explorer, scholar, writer and translator Sir Richard Burton – who, although he lived a relatively dangerous life, lived to be honored with a knighthood bestowed by Queen Victoria and die at a relatively advanced age.

The character of Madam Candelaria was based on a real woman, Andrea Castañón Villanueva, who may have been present in the Alamo during the siege and nursed the very ill James Bowie. She was among a number of other women recorded to have been present, mostly wives, mothers and sisters of members of the Texian and Tejano garrison. She and her second husband did keep a dance hall in San Antonio, and she was renowned for her charitable work. Whether she was a survivor of the Alamo siege or not can't be confirmed to the absolute satisfaction of historians, but toward the end of her life she was awarded a small pension by the Texas Legislature on that ground, and for her charitable work of nursing during later smallpox epidemic.

The Third Adventure – The Haunting of Bell House

There is or was no Bell House in 19th century Galveston, supposedly built on the site of Jean Lafitte's "Campeche" pirate colony, although Lafitte did have a house – supposedly painted red, called La Maison Rouge, and headquarters for his privateering and smuggling enterprise from 1817-1820, until wrecked by a hurricane and chased away by the fledgling US Navy on a mission to eradicate piracy along the Gulf Coat. Modern-day historians say that the Maison Rouge was at 1417 Harborside Drive, where a historical marker noting the site is located, although the visible ruins there are from a much later house. The site is allegedly haunted – and of course wherever pirates have been, stories of their buried treasure abound.

The Fourth Adventure – The Death of a Disagreeable Man

Edward Balfour is based on a historical character to whom I took an immediate dislike on reading about him in Alvin Josephy's *The Civil War In The West*: John Robert Baylor, a nephew of the Baylor for whom the university is named. John Baylor lived through several militia actions during the time of the Republic of Texas and survived the Civil War. Surprisingly, he lived to the age of 71 and died of natural causes. This may have come to a surprise to many who knew him in life, as he had made many, many enemies, Indian, Anglo and Texan. He was sacked by Jefferson Davis as a Confederate military governor in the New Mexico Territory for having, among other things, ordered the distribution of poisoned foodstuffs to Apache Indians – this at the very time when the Confederate government was attempting to make allies of other Indian tribes in the West. Baylor continued to have a reputation as a man with a violent temper; he is supposed to have killed a man in a feud over livestock and been involved in at least one gunfight. But he was not poisoned with a tincture brewed from oleander, a hardy decorative shrub from South America much planted across the south and west, which was imported through Galveston at about this time. All parts of the oleander – leaves, blossoms, twigs and all – are deathly poisonous. Even the smoke from burning oleander stems and foliage is dangerous.

However, Robert S. Neighbors, who also featured in this adventure and others was a real person, a native Virginian. He sought adventure and fortune in Texas in the fateful spring of 1836, when he was just twenty-one. He found adventure, all right, serving in the Republic of Texas' tiny professional army as quartermaster. Eventually, he gravitated to San Antonio and another kind of military service as a member of Jack Hays' volunteer Ranger company. When the Mexican Army under General Adrian Woll made a lightning-fast raid on San Antonio in September 1842, Bob Neighbors was one of those taken captive and packed off into Mexico for a stint of imprisonment in the San Carlos Fortress – Perote Prison. After two years there, he returned to Texas and became the Indian agent with primary responsibility for the peoples of two tribes noted for volunteering as guides and combatants with the Rangers – the Lipan Apache and the Tonkawa. Both these tribes were traditional enemies of the Comanche. Neighbors developed a fluency in the various languages, a grasp on the subtleties of tribal cultures – and more importantly, the friendship of many. It was said of him at the time that no white man in Texas had more friends or a greater influence among the Tribes. He was a good friend of Old Owl of the Penateka Comanche – and was one of the negotiators at the peace conference which led to a peace treaty between the Penateka Comanche and the German settlers who arrived on the Texas frontier through the auspices of the Mainzer Adelsverein.

John Baylor, who had been one of Neighbors' sub-agents in spite of his detestation of Indians, became one of Neighbors' most bitter enemies, and never missed the opportunity of inciting the anger of white settlers against the Reservation Indians. At one point, Bob Neighbors had to call on federal troops stationed at Camp Cooper and Fort Belknap, to protect the Reservation against an attack by white vigilantes – vigilantes led by John Baylor. By late 1859, Neighbors realized that his Indian charges were no longer safe in Texas. He organized the evacuation of the Brazos reservations, and personally escorted them to a new federal reservation in present-day Oklahoma. He achieved this without any loss of life, but on his return to Fort Belknap to file his final report as the superintendent of Indian affairs, he was shot down from behind, in retaliation for his friendship and championship of the Indians. He was buried in the Fort Belknap cemetery.

John S. "Rip" Ford, who also appears briefly in this adventure was another real and slightly larger-than life personality. Like John Baylor, he lived a long and adventurous life, and against all expectation, died in bed at the age of 82, almost making it into the 20th century. He had also survived service in two wars and innumerable campaigns along the borders and against various hostile Indian tribes, several rounds of frontier exploration, election to public office... and as a newspaper editor, in the days when public discourse was conducted metaphorically with a set of brass knuckles.

He arrived in Texas in 1836 at the age of 21, Texas's War of Independence by a bare month - about the last significant historical event in Texas that John S. Ford would miss. At the end of his life, he was working on a memoir which would fairly double as a history of Texas in the 19th century. Having studied medicine with a doctor in Tennessee, he hung out his shingle in the settlement of San Augustine. For some years, he also served as a volunteer Ranger with a series of local companies including one commanded by Jack Hays. He also taught himself law. Then he got into politics and gave up medicine for the newspaper business. He picked up the nickname "Rip" when he served the company of Rangers that Jack Hays recruited to serve alongside the American army in the Mexican war. When the war ended, it seemed that the peacetime business of running a newspaper had palled; Ford sold the paper, and went with Robert Neighbors, to explore a route across the southwest to El Paso. Gold had been discovered in California that very year, and an overland route to California via Austin and El Paso would prove profitable. Then he raised a company of Rangers to patrol the border. When Texas seceded from the Union, he was commissioned as a colonel to raise a command and take over the Union Army's forts and commands between Brownsville and El Paso. Ford was off into the field, fighting an assortment of enemies; the Yankees, renegade Indians, and Mexican outlaws. His command fought the very last land fight of the Civil War, in May of 1864 at Palmito Ranch, nearly a month after Lee's surrender at Appomattox. Very ill at the end of that war, he eventually recovered enough to continue involvement in state politics, and writing for various publications. He himself was elected mayor of Brownsville, and state senator, and appointed as superintendent for the state institution for the deaf. He transformed it into a school, rather than an asylum, and took enormous pride in the progress of its' students and graduates, until reoccurring ill-health forced him to resign. He spent his last years writing memoirs and news stories and being interviewed by other history buffs. He had written his memoirs, and gotten a fair way into an ambitious, eye-witness history of Texas from 1836 to 1886. Among modern historians, he and Winston Churchill shared a most unique facility for having made almost as much history as they wrote.

The Fifth Adventure – Two Houses, Alike in Dignity
The two main antagonists of this adventure, Richard Bullock and Angelina Eberly were real people – and as outlined in this story, did maintain rival hospitality establishments in Austin during this period. Richard Bullock is mainly famous for the so-called Pig War, which was not actually an honest-to-Pete real shooting war. It did involve the government of the Republic of Texas and the diplomatic representative of France; a gentleman-dandy named Jean Pierre Isidore Dubois de Saligny who called himself the Comte de Saligny, who had been instrumental in recommending that France extend diplomatic recognition to the Republic of Texas. Unfortunately, Dubois turned out to be terribly undiplomatic – possibly utterly appalled at arriving in the new

capital city of Austin, a ramble of hastily built frame shacks and log cabins scattered along a series of muddy streets along the scenic and wooded shores of the upper Colorado River. Dubois arrived with two French servants, including a chef, a very fine collection of wines, elegant furniture and household goods; a man of culture and refinement – and ill-unprepared for the raw crudities of the Texas frontier. At first, Dubois took rooms at Richard Bullock's hotel. Bullock also kept a herd of pigs which were allowed to roam freely, and eat what they could scavenge, along the muddy streets and in back of the frame buildings and log cabins set up to do the business of the Republic. Eventually, Dubois, rented a small building nearby to use as an office and residence while a fine new legation was being built. He was most particularly plagued by Bullock's pigs, breaking through the fence around his garden, and even into his house, where they ate some bedclothes and papers.

Furious, Dubois instructed one of his servants to kill any pigs found on the property that he had rented, which was done. Richard Bullock, outraged, demanded payment for his loss, which was indignantly refused on the grounds of diplomatic immunity. The matter escalated when Bullock encountered Dubois' swine-killing servant one day in the street and thrashed him. An official protest was filed, and a hearing ordered by the Texas Secretary of State. Citing international law, Dubois refused to attend or allow his servant to testify. Richard Bullock was freed on bail. When Dubois complained bitterly to Republic authorities about this, he was told that he could collect his passport and depart at any time. He left in a huff and stayed away for a year, never actually living in the elegant residence described here. The house, now the French Legation was eventually rented to Archbishop Odin, and then sold to another owner who used it as a school for many years. It still stands today, the only structure remaining from that period. Richard Bullock became the toast of the town, and his pigs celebrities, for of course the story got around. The fracas also put an end to a generous loan from France and plans to bring 8,000 French settlers to settle on Texas lands – as well as a military alliance that would allow stationing of French garrisons in Texas to protect them.

Twice-wed and twice widowed, Angelina Belle Peyton Eberly was born in Sumner County, Tennessee.. She and her first husband, John Peyton (who was also her first cousin) settled in San Felipe-on-the-Brazos, the de facto capitol of the American settlements in Texas. They opened and ran an inn, before John died in 1834. She carried on with running it, until the War of Independence broke out two years later. Sam Houston, the one leader among the Texans who kept his head, ordered that all the Texan settlements be destroyed and their residents evacuate to the east. His scratch army fell back and back, until they turned and fought at San Jacinto – and won.

In the aftermath of the war, Angelina Peyton took her family to Columbia on the Brazos, which would for a time be the capitol of Texas. Late in 1836, she married again, to a widower named Jacob Eberly. Within three years, she and Jacob had moved to Austin, on the far settled frontier of Texas, but square in the middle of the territory claimed by the Republic. The place had been chosen by the second President of the Republic, Mirabeau Lamar. Angelina and Jacob opened a boarding house – the Eberly House, catering to members of the new Legislature, and to those officers of Lamar's administration.

Everyone agreed that Austin had a fine and prosperous future: within the first year of being laid out, the population had gone from a handful of families to nearly 1,000. The Eberly House was considered very fine: even Sam Houston, upon being elected President after Lamar, preferred living there, rather than the presidential mansion. Jacob Eberly died in 1841. The following year, war with Mexico threatened again; Sam Houston decreed that the Legislature should meet in Washington-on-the-Brazos. He felt it too dangerous to meet in Austin, and he had never been as enthusiastic about Austin as Lamar had been. Panic emptied Austin, as the population fell. Government and private buildings stood empty, while a handful of die-hard residents carried on, hoping that when things calmed down, the Legislature would return. The archives of the State of Texas were stored in the General Land Office Building. A committee of vigilance formed, to ensure that the records remained, after President Houston politely requested their removal to East Texas.

In the dead of night on December 29th, 1842, a party of men acting under Houston's direction arrived, with orders to remove the archives in secret and without shedding any blood. Unfortunately, they were rather noisy about loading the wagons. Angelina Eberly woke, looked out of a window and immediately realized what was going on. She ran outside and fired off the six-pound cannon that the residents kept loaded with grapeshot in case of an Indian attack. The shot alerted the vigilance committee and supposedly punched a hole in the side of the General Land Office Building. The men fled with three wagons full of documents, pursued within hours by the volunteers of the vigilance committee, who caught up with them the next day. The archives were returned. Sam Houston was admonished by the Legislature for trying to relocate the capitol.

The Legislature returned to Austin in 1845. After annexation by the United States, it would be the state capitol. Angelina Eberly, who had fired the shot that ensured it would do so, moved her hotel business to Indianola, the Queen City of the Gulf coast. She did not marry again, and ran a profitable and well-frequented hotel, until her death in 1860.